"I'm not asking forgiveness."

Of course he wasn't. Luca wasn't a man who cared for the good opinion of others. What did it matter to Luca Cavallaro how Mia felt about him? His sense of self was far too assured for her feelings to have any impact.

"Then what are you asking for? What do you want from me?" She lifted a hand to his chest. "What do you want from me?" she repeated, groaning, because she'd been going crazy with wanting him and suddenly, she didn't care about anything except the fact he was here and seemed to need her as she needed him.

"One week." He pushed her backward, pressing his body to her, so she was caught between the edge of her desk and his strong thighs, and her world began to crumble and tumble and roll, her eyes filled with stars and fireworks and flame. "Give me one week of your time, Mia. Let me have you, just for one week."

Brooding Billionaire Brothers

Passionate, commanding, irresistible!

Billionaire half brothers Luca Cavallaro and Max Stone may have had very different childhoods, but blood is thicker than water. These powerful men are much more alike than they want to admit— besides from being infamous in the business world for their ruthlessness, their ice-cold hearts are also completely untouchable! That is, until they meet the only women to thaw them...

The Sicilian's Deal for "I Do"

Luca Cavallaro may have left Mia Marini at the altar twelve months earlier, but she's haunted his dreams ever since...and now he wants to claim her for the wedding night they never had!

Available now!

Contracted and Claimed by the Boss

Paige Cooper was looking to escape her celebrity status, not run straight into a contract that could bind her forever to brooding billionaire Max Stone...

Coming soon!

HARLEQUIN®
PRESENTS™

Recycling programs for this product may not exist in your area.

ISBN-13: 978-1-335-59232-3

The Sicilian's Deal for "I Do"

Copyright © 2024 by Clare Connelly

Harlequin Enterprises ULC
22 Adelaide St. West, 41st Floor
Toronto, Ontario M5H 4E3, Canada
www.Harlequin.com

Printed in U.S.A.

Clare Connelly

THE SICILIAN'S DEAL FOR "I DO"

Clare Connelly was raised in small-town Australia among a family of avid readers. She spent much of her childhood up a tree, Harlequin book in hand. Clare is married to her own real-life hero, and they live in a bungalow near the sea with their two children. She is frequently found staring into space—a surefire sign she is in the world of her characters. She has a penchant for French food and ice-cold champagne, and Harlequin novels continue to be her favorite-ever books. Writing for Harlequin Presents is a long-held dream. Clare can be contacted via clareconnelly.com or on her Facebook page.

Books by Clare Connelly

Harlequin Presents

Emergency Marriage to the Greek
Pregnant Princess in Manhattan
The Boss's Forbidden Assistant
Twelve Nights in the Prince's Bed

Passionately Ever After...

Cinderella in the Billionaire's Castle

The Cinderella Sisters

Vows on the Virgin's Terms
Forbidden Nights in Barcelona

The Long-Lost Cortéz Brothers

The Secret She Must Tell the Spaniard
Desert King's Forbidden Temptation

Visit the Author Profile page
at Harlequin.com for more titles.

PROLOGUE

Twelve months earlier

BENEATH THE CHAPEL WINDOW, in the small square tucked deep in the ancient heart of Palermo, the world kept turning. Children ran by, gelatos in hand, sun on their chubby cheeks, parents walking behind them arm in arm, smiling, doting, adoring.

Mia watched as a boy of about nine tucked behind a wall, grinning, waiting until his sister, perhaps six, walked near to him, when he jumped out and shouted something. Though the chapel glass was thin and rippled by age, Mia couldn't hear through it, but she guessed it was something like, 'Boo!' The girl jumped, then both keeled over, laughing.

Despite the anxiety building inside Mia's gut over her own situation, she smiled. A weak, distracted smile, before she turned her back on the outside world with deep reluctance.

'Surely he's just been delayed.'

She caught sight of herself in an ancient mirror. Like the windows, it too was damaged by the passage of time, so it distorted her slightly, but that didn't matter. The ludicrousness of this was all too apparent, even without a clear reflection.

Had she really thought this would happen?

That today would be her wedding day?

That Luca Cavallaro would *actually* marry her?

Flashes of their brief, whirlwind courtship ran before her eyes. Her bewilderment at the idea of marriage, her parents' explanation that it was best for the family, for the business, and then, meeting Luca, who had swept her away with a single look, a brooding, fulminating glance that had turned her blood to lava and made her wonder if she'd ever really existed before knowing him.

Every time they'd been together, she'd felt that same zing. When they'd touched—even just the lightest brushing of hands—it had been like fireworks igniting in her bloodstream, and their kiss, that one, wild kiss, had left Mia with the certainty that she was born to be held by him.

The hot sting of tears threatened but Mia sucked in a calming breath, refusing to give into the temptation to weep. Not here, not now, certainly not in front of her parents, who were staring at Mia with expressions of abject disappointment, and, worse, a lack of surprise. As if they had almost expected this, for her to fail them.

'What did you say to him?' Jennifer Marini pushed, arms crossed over her svelte frame. 'You were alone with him, by the car the other night. What happened?'

Unlike Mia, Jennifer was tall and willow thin—a difference Jennifer never failed to highlight. Instead of growing into a stunning, svelte woman, like Jennifer, Mia had stopped growing a little over five feet, and had developed lush, generous curves. *Just like your mother*, Jennifer had never failed to condemn, as if bearing a resemblance to the woman who'd birthed Mia was a sin.

Reluctantly, Mia's eyes were drawn back to her own reflection. To the frothy white dress and ridiculous hairstyle. She'd been primped and preened and pulled in a thousand directions since first light. An army of women had worked on getting her 'bride ready'. She thought of the waxing with heated cheeks and blinked again quickly now.

Despite their efforts, Mia couldn't help thinking how far this was from her best look. She was under no illusions as to her beauty. She was pretty enough, she supposed, in the right light and to the right person, and as long as she could remember her biological mother's eyes and smile, Mia felt glad that they lived on in her own face. But she liked pasta far too much and disliked sweating generally, which ruled out a vast array of cardio exercises. She was never going to be reed thin like her adoptive mother, nor did she want to be. There was a sternness to Jennifer, and a general lack of *joie de vivre* that Mia had always associated with her restrictive diet: far better to eat the pasta—and the gelato and the focaccia and the mozzarella—and be happy, Mia always thought.

'I—nothing,' she said, quickly, even though memories of those snatched moments were making her pulse rush now.

'I did everything I could for you,' Jennifer said with a ticking of her finger to her palm, the harsh red of her manicure catching Mia's eye. 'I did everything I could to pave the way for this marriage. You must have said something.'

'I haven't spoken to him in a week,' Mia denied. Perhaps it was strange not to talk to your fiancé for so long, but then, this was far from a normal marriage, and her situation was far from normal. Marriage to Luca Cavallaro wasn't a love match. Not for him, anyway. She frowned, and her heart began to beat faster, to race, as she remembered their first meeting. The way their eyes had locked, and something had shifted inside her, a part of Mia she hadn't known existed, the part of her she'd always wondered about.

Whatever physical beauty she lacked, he made up for, with abundance.

Like a specimen from a gallery or a famous actor or a pristine example of what the male species *should* be. Tall, sculpted, muscular without being bulky, strong, and when he'd looked at her, she'd felt this giddy sense of disbelief that *he* was actually going to be her husband.

They'd only seen each other a handful of times after that, always with Mia's parents until that last night, and the conversations had revolved around the businesses. The sale of Mia's father's old family corporation to Luca Cavallaro and his newly minted multibillion-dollar fortune. Just what the world needed: another beyond handsome, alpha-male billionaire!

But then there'd been *that* kiss, when he'd been leaving one evening and Jennifer had hastily told Mia to walk him out. The moon had been high in the sky above her parents' estate in the countryside surrounding Palermo, the sound of the ocean drowned out by the rushing of her blood as he'd pulled her into his arms, stared down at her, frowned for a moment and then, he'd simply kissed her, as though it were the most natural thing in the world.

Perhaps it was. They'd spent hours in each other's company over the course of their engagement—maybe he'd expected more kissing, more of everything? Mia didn't know. That night, he'd taken matters into his own hands... She'd expected it would turn out like a movie, a three-second kiss, maximum, but his lips had lingered, and the world had slowed right down along with it. She'd moaned, because he'd smelled so good but tasted better; the kiss was by far the best thing she'd ever felt. Like coming home—except, Mia had never really felt at home anywhere since her parents had died.

And then his arms had tightened around her back, melding her curvy body to his, and he'd deepened the kiss, his passionate inspection of her mouth leaving her shaking, writhing wantonly against him, until he'd pulled away and stared down at her once more. Was that surprise in his features? At the time, Mia had thought so, but, like all memories, it shifted and morphed so she couldn't have said with any confidence the next morning that it hadn't been boredom. Or worse, disgust. After all, Mia had very limited experience with kissing men.

That had been one week before their wedding. They hadn't seen nor spoken to one another afterwards, but she'd had no reason to doubt him.

No reason to doubt this would come to pass. If anything, the kiss had cemented his intentions for Mia. How could he make her feel like that and then walk away?

She could have wept when she thought of her childish fantasies, the dreams that had kept her awake at night and stirred her body to a fever pitch of wanting.

When her parents had first told her about the wedding, she'd been unsure about the idea. They'd wanted to know a Marini would still work in the family business, and also that Mia would be taken care of once they'd sold off such a valuable asset. But it didn't take long for Mia to warm to the idea.

Of no longer being a Marini, which, in some ways, she'd never really felt herself to be.

Of no longer being alone.

Of being a wife, married—and to someone like Luca. Putting aside his physical beauty, he was rich and powerful and she was sure she'd be able to lead her own life while living under his roof, that he wouldn't trouble himself with her comings and goings. But also, there would be children, and that thought alone had made her a very willing accomplice to the whole scheme. Children, a family of her own, something she'd so desperately wanted since losing her parents and the sense of security that came from knowing she was loved.

Though she was outwardly compliant with her adoptive parents, a streak of rebellion had been growing inside Mia, and marrying Luca Cavallaro seemed like a brilliant way to exercise her independence, finally.

'He's probably just late,' Mia murmured, trying to reassure herself.

'To his own wedding?' Jennifer demanded, moving one of the red-taloned hands to her hips. 'He is supposed to be out there, waiting for you, Mia. That's the way it works.'

'He's a very busy and important man,' Mia pointed out. 'That's why we're here, isn't it?'

Gianni Marini shook his head, his rounded face showing obvious impatience. 'All you had to do was sit in the corner and smile from time to time.'

Something sparked in Mia's chest. Had she done something wrong? Had she been the one to ruin this? Had the kiss been so bad? She spun away again quickly, trying to find the same family with the brother and sister playing hide and seek, but they were gone. The light danced off the large tree in the centre of the square. Mia had always loved the light of Palermo. She'd hated leaving it to go to milky grey England, but

Jennifer had insisted that her daughter attend her alma mater, so boarding school it had been. How she'd missed the sunshine and sea salt.

'Oh, God.' Jennifer's voice crackled in the air. Mia closed her eyes without turning around. She'd been holding onto hope, remembering Luca's eyes, absolutely certain that someone with such beautiful eyes and the ability to truly look at someone and *see* them could never do anything quite so callous as this. But then, she also knew. Even as the hairdressers had worked and the make-up artist had glued false lashes in place and her nails had been painted and made hot beneath a UV light, Mia had somehow *known* it would all come to nothing.

'What is it?' Gianni asked loudly.

'He's not coming.'

'How do you know?'

'The whole world knows,' Jennifer snapped. 'Look.' Mia kept her eyes shut, back to the room, breath silenced despite the heaviness of her heart.

Gianni read aloud, quickly, '"*Runaway Groom*"—that's the headline. *"It appears Luca Cavallaro preferred the idea of an airport runway to that of a wedding aisle after all. The billionaire bachelor was spotted leaving Italy last night despite his planned wedding, which was to take place today, to Mia Marini, daughter of steel magnate Gianni Marini. Trouble in corporate merger paradise? Watch this space.'"*

Mia groaned, the last sentence almost the hardest to hear of all, because she realised that the whole world knew their marriage was just a corporate merger. And it was. But was it so implausible to think a man like Luca might actually want to marry Mia for herself?

A single tear slid down her cheek.

'He left last night!' Jennifer barked, her voice trembling with rage. 'And didn't have the decency to tell us. All of this, all of this trouble, and not even a chance to save face. How could he do this to us, Gianni?'

To you? Mia wanted to scream. She was the one in the ridiculous dress with awful hair and over-the-top make-up. Suddenly, she was claustrophobic and couldn't breathe. Could barely stand up. Stars danced behind her eyes and she spun wildly, staring at her parents without seeing them, then locating the door to the small room.

'I have to go.'

'Go where, Mia?' Jennifer asked sharply.

'Outside. Anywhere. I don't care. I just—I can't breathe.'

'Mia, don't,' her mother warned, but too late. Mia burst into the chapel, to a packed room of people, all there for the spectacle of this. Most were on their phones, but when she appeared, they looked up, almost as one, some with pity, others with a delighted sense of *schadenfreude*. Mia barely noticed any of it. She scrambled along the back of the church, past the guests who'd not been able to find seats, ignoring their words, their voices, throwing open the heavy, old timber doors so the beautiful Palermo light bathed her. She closed her eyes and let it make her strong for a moment, then ran down the stairs and across the square, right into a child who smeared strawberry gelato against the horrible white dress.

And all Mia could do was stand still, in the middle of the square, hands on her hips, head tilted to the sky, and laugh. There was nothing else for it.

CHAPTER ONE

NOT A SINGLE day went past between then and now in which Luca Cavallaro wasn't convinced he did the right thing. He couldn't think of the Marini family without a sense of ruthless anger and disgust.

They'd lied to him.

They'd tried to sell him a worthless business with clever accounting and incomplete statements. And to tie him up in marriage to their daughter. Worse, Luca had come damned close to going along with it. Luca Cavallaro, who'd known from almost as long as he could walk and talk that he never wanted to marry, never wanted to love. Not after seeing what love could do to a person.

Then again, this hadn't been about love, so much as a necessary term to secure a company that had come to mean a lot to Luca. His hand formed a fist at his side as he remembered how he'd felt when he'd first heard that Marini Enterprises was available…the company his father had coveted but failed to secure. Luca would stop at nothing to make it his. Not because he cared about earning his father's approval, but because he was driven to win, at all costs, and if he could beat his father, so much the better.

So he'd accepted the marriage deal as part of the merger, had even started to relish the idea of marriage to Mia Marini. It wouldn't be a real marriage, after all, just a convenient union— but there would have been some definite perks. In fact, he'd started to look forward to having Mia in his home, and his bed. That wasn't the same as marrying for love—there had been no risk to either of them.

But then, he'd learned the truth: that the Marinis were trying to swindle him. The company his own father had fought tooth and nail to buy ten years earlier had become practically worthless. Did the older Marini really think Luca was so stupid? That he wouldn't undertake more due diligence than the average person?

His team of forensic accountants had been raking over Marini corporate documents for more than a month and finally found evidence of Gianni's deception, of the true state of Marini Enterprises. It was almost bankrupt. Using an admittedly clever scheme of shadow companies and trusts, he'd been able to make it look profitable and successful in order to lure a buyer, but it was all a façade.

Just like Mia.

Outrage had filled every cell of his body. It wasn't just the money, it was that they'd taken him for a fool who would believe their lies. It wasn't as if Luca craved anyone's approval, least of all his father's, but in the back of his mind there'd been the knowledge that Carrick Stone was waiting for Luca to fail, to come back to Australia with his tail between his legs. The Marini family wouldn't have ruined him—Luca was too wealthy—but he would have been mortified for the truth to come out, and for his father to know. And so he'd left, without a backwards glance.

And yet…

In the warm, afternoon sun, standing near the edge of his infinity pool, Luca reached for his phone once more, his eyes landing immediately on the article, to the photo of Mia standing, smiling sweetly, beside a man Luca had met on a handful of occasions. Lorenzo di Angelo had inherited the responsibility of running his family's textile business, based out of Milano, but in the last few years he'd been launching an impressive move into the south, and wider across Europe. Luca had been watching with interest—he watched all business expansion with interest, having an almost savant-like ability to track the landscape of corporate movements across the world.

So, Gianni had found another investor.

And Mia was going along with it, just like before, a willing lure to the next mark.

Mia Marini engaged—again!

Even though he didn't regret walking away from their deal, something about the headline left a stain of discomfort in his chest, and he couldn't say why. Mia had gone along with her parents' scheme. She worked for the business; she was undoubtedly complicit in their lies. And yet, the media coverage of their failed wedding had all focused on her. Jilted. Ditched. The photo of her in the square, the dress covered in ice cream, a child staring at her with wonder as she'd looked at the sky, face scrunched, lips parted.

Shame had been a blade at his side, even when he knew he'd done the right thing, even when he knew she deserved it. He'd ignored calls from his father—as if Carrick had any right to lecture Luca about any damned thing—and his half-brother, Max. Though that was much harder to do, given the affection and respect he felt for Max Stone. But he hadn't wanted to answer questions about the marriage, nor about the Marini business, and the fact he'd left Mia to clean up the mess after he'd discovered the truth.

And hadn't she deserved that?

She'd gone along with it all. She could have told him the truth, especially on that night, by the car, but she hadn't. That kiss… He closed his eyes as he remembered, as pleasure vibrated through his body in a way that still had the power to shake him. What had he thought? That a kiss like that was somehow an unlocking of her soul? That she would be honest with him because of the desire that exploded between them?

There was too much at stake for honesty.

She'd been a willing piece in the whole scam, had even been willing to sell herself into the deal, to marry a man she didn't know, to get him to shore up a worthless company.

That made her almost the guiltiest of all.

After the wedding of the century that wasn't, Mia Marini is trying again, this time with the oldest son of the di Angelos, bringing together two of Italy's most established families.

Well, good for Mia. She'd duped another guy into the scheme.

He placed his phone down on the table, moving to the edge of the pool and staring now at the crystal-clear water that led all the way to the tiled edge, and beyond it, to the immaculate Sicilian waters.

She'd been an irrelevancy at first.

And then, she'd kissed him—or he'd kissed her—and a spark of desire had ignited into something far more powerful.

She'd been his fiancée.

He could have taken her if he'd wanted, and suddenly, he had wanted. He'd wanted to fold her into the back of the car and drive away from her parents and their estate, drive anywhere there was a big, comfortable bed, and make love to her, to hear her moan a little more like she had, to have her cry out his name.

He didn't need to go back to his phone, to look at the photo. He could see Mia in his mind, as she'd been that night beneath the milky moonlight, and as she was in the picture, with di Angelo. He dived into the water as a resolution formed firmly in his mind. Less a resolution, he thought with powerful strokes, but a need to possess what was, at one time, his. Or should have been.

He'd walked away that night because he'd been angry with her, angry that she'd lied to him, angry she'd tried to dupe him, then kissing him like that.

He was still angry.

But the Sicilian blood ran hot in his veins and it demanded something of Luca that he could no longer deny: before Mia married anyone else, before she willingly sold herself to another man for the sake of her family's crumbling empire, she would be his.

All his, just as she'd pledged to him when they'd become engaged, and as her body had promised that night when they'd kissed beneath the moonlight. Something had been ignited between them, something urgent and intense. He'd been able to ignore it until now, until reading that Mia was about to marry someone else, and he would lose the ability to act on this desire once and for all. With a new sense of resolve, he cut through the water, temptation finally something he intended to obey.

Ostensibly, the ball was a way to honour her parents. Each year, the Marini family hosted this event, a fundraiser for her parents' charity, but for Mia, it simply drew attention to how alone she was. Despite her newly announced engagement, despite her parents' professed love for her—it all felt like an elaborate lie! She was marrying a man she barely knew and certainly didn't love, who'd made it clear he intended to be a free agent right up until they signed on the dotted line—which was fine by Mia, she was under no illusion as to the kind of marriage they'd have.

But on top of that, she'd been raised by parents who'd taken her in out of a duty to her biological mother—her adoptive mother's oldest friend—and who'd found themselves steadily disappointed by Mia as she'd grown. Somewhere deep down, Mia was sure they did love her, in their own way, and certain that they wanted the best for her, but it hadn't been a happy childhood and even now the shadows of those years reached into her life and dulled her view of things.

Nights like this made it worse, because she was forced to remember what life had been like before. With her parents.

She'd only been young when they'd died but core memories of their happiness and love were imprinted on her soul. Was it any wonder her greatest fantasy in life was of having a family of her own? Of having children she could adore and spoil, and pour all of her love into, finally?

'I thought they'd be here,' her mother hissed through clenched teeth, eyes darting to Gianni's face, skin pale. 'Where are they?'

Standing beside them in the crowded bar, Mia leaned closer to hear.

'A scheduling conflict. Don't worry, Jennifer. This wedding—and merger—will go ahead. This time, it's different.'

Mia's eyes briefly swept shut. The di Angelos. Her gut twisted with doubts and uncertainties, at the idea that her second attempt at marriage might be as ill-fated as the first, but then, no. It wasn't possible. Lorenzo was nothing like Luca. Where there was something dangerous about Luca's brilliant genius and ruthless determination, and certainly about his unfettered sex appeal, Lorenzo was calm, methodical and not at all sexually attracted to Mia, which put her at ease. They'd calmly discussed the merger, their reason for marrying, his intention to continue to date discreetly until they were officially married. Which was just how Mia wanted it.

'They know how important this night is to us. The media will be wondering—'

'The media does not matter,' he interrupted sharply. 'Now stop worrying and smile. People are looking.'

Sure enough, some people were looking in their direction, or were they? Eyes that were pointed their way were, on closer inspection, focused ever so slightly beyond them, so Mia threw a glance over her shoulder and then shivered, for no reason she could think of.

'Excuse me,' she murmured to her parents, nonetheless unnerved and deciding she needed a sip of champagne and a quiet moment.

'Where are you going?'

'To mingle,' she lied, flashing a smile at her father. 'I won't be long.'

Disapproval flattened Jennifer's lips but Mia had long since given up trying to guess what she'd done to upset her adoptive mother. She turned her back and disappeared into the crowd before Jennifer could invent a reason for her to stay.

Whether the di Angelos were there or not, the night was a success. Mia could tell by how many guests were in attendance, and by the calibre of celebrities. The event had drawn a host of well-heeled, monied glitterati and that meant the charity would benefit. She was glad, though no one observing Mia would have realised it, if they'd looked at her serious expression.

At the bar, she waited in line, and finally, at the front, ordered a glass of champagne, gripped it with relief and began to cut through the crowd once more, nodding politely when she saw an acquaintance or someone her parents knew, until she reached the doors that led to the rooftop garden. The night was warm, and so there wasn't as much privacy out here as Mia had craved, but she remembered a small corner that offered a little more seclusion and she moved there, glad to find it unoccupied. She could sit on one of the chairs and remove her painfully high heels, reaching down to massage the ligaments of her ankles with relief. Above her, fairy lights had been strung from edge to edge of the rooftop garden, giving it a magical feel, interspersed as they were with potted plants. The sound of happy conversations swirled around her from the elegant guests, giving Mia a sense of anonymity—compounded by the two enormous ferns that shielded her from view.

When her champagne was half empty, she wondered how much longer she could reasonably hide out here for. Would anyone be missing her?

A wry smile tipped her lips.

Her parents' initial impatience with her disappearance would have dissipated in the face of the success of the event, and Jennifer was no doubt in there enjoying the attention of her well-heeled friends. Which meant Mia had at least the rest of her champagne glass to go...

She leaned back a little in the chair, closed her eyes, breathed deeply and tried to relax, to tell herself that she was making the right decisions in life, even when doubts often chased her. If her parents had lived, what would they say about this marriage?

Her smile turned into a grimace and then a sigh as she sipped her champagne.

If her parents had lived, she'd have never been in this situation—forced to seek an escape from adoptive parents who both loved and resented her, who showed their love by being way too protective and controlling, and for whom Mia had been conditioned to have such a high level of gratitude that she could never countermand them.

The rational part of Mia's brain knew how stupid that was, wondered why she didn't just tell them that she didn't want to work in the family business, that she didn't want to marry a stranger just to retain an interest in Marini Enterprises. But the little girl who'd been rescued from foster care was told over and over again how lucky she was to have them, couldn't defy their wishes. So the best she could do was try to make her own wishes accord with theirs.

And in Lorenzo, perhaps she'd succeeded?

She sighed again, lifted her champagne flute to her lips, then glanced left when a sudden motion caught her eye.

And felt as though every cell in her body had reverberated to fever pitch then stopped altogether.

She jerked to standing, spilling champagne on the tiled ground in a dramatic splashing motion, shock rendering her body capable of only staccato movements.

'Luca?' She blinked rapidly, sure her eyes were deceiving her.

But then his lips curled in that smile she remembered so well, half cynicism, half seduction, and her stomach rolled so hard she thought it might fly out of her body.

'What are you doing here?' she demanded, unable to resist wiping a hand across her eyes in case this was a fantasy.

'It is a charity event. I bought a ticket.'

'You bought a ticket,' she parroted, eyes huge. 'Erm, why?'

He shrugged indolently. 'Why not? I have the money.'

'But this is my *parents'* charity,' she said quickly, lifting her champagne glass and draining it completely.

'So it is.'

Her lips parted with indignation. 'You shouldn't be here.'

He watched her with such a look of relaxation that she was sure it was fake. Either that, or he truly didn't care about the way he'd humiliated her and upended her life, not to mention the pain he'd caused her parents. The gall of him to appear like this, wearing a tuxedo and looking so damned gorgeous. How dared he? Next minute, he'd tell her he was here with some supermodel or something. Grinding her teeth, she flashed him a look that was pure resentment.

'I mean it, Luca. You need to leave.'

Instead, he took a step closer. Mia braced. Waves of heat seemed to rush towards her, radiating from his body, reminding her of when they'd first met and she'd been so completely overwhelmed by him and her desire for him. She squeezed her champagne glass more tightly, wishing it had magical refilling capabilities.

'Why?'

She was at a loss for words. Shaking her head, she finally said, 'Isn't that obvious?'

'Not to me.'

'You…you…you left me on our wedding day!' she spluttered, then quickly looked around to make sure no one had witnessed her outburst. She lifted her fingertips to her forehead, tried to remember that it had been a year ago, that she was different now, that her whole life was different. Not only that, his treatment of Mia had made her stronger, smarter, had forced her to really take control of her life. To an outsider, it might appear that nothing had changed—after all, she was entering into another arranged marriage—but her eyes were wide open this time. She was nobody's fool. This marriage would be all on her terms.

'Yes,' he agreed, taking another step towards her. Why wouldn't Mia's feet work to draw her backwards? 'But that does not mean I haven't thought about you.'

Her lips parted, the statement striking her in the chest like a bolt of lightning. It was a lie.

It had to be a lie. She placed her champagne flute down on the nearby table with unnecessary force.

'Oh? Thinking what a first-rate bastard you were?'

His eyes narrowed imperceptibly. 'Of opportunities wasted.' He moved closer still, so close she could smell his aftershave and feel his warmth, and her insides jerked accordingly. 'I have been thinking of that night.'

'What night?' she asked in a strangled voice, taking a step back until she connected with the stone wall behind her. She was grateful for the support at first, but then Luca moved forward and effectively trapped her, his frame so much larger than hers, so it was impossible to imagine how she could escape. Only—she could. If she told him to go away, firmly, she was pretty sure he would.

So why didn't she?

Why didn't she stamp on his foot, for good measure, then tell him to get lost?

Her mouth was dry. The simple act of swallowing seemed to require a monumental effort.

'Do you need a reminder?'

His gaze dropped to her lips and Mia's heart felt as though it might leap out of her chest, ribs be damned. 'No,' she said quickly. 'That's fine.'

His smirk showed scepticism. 'Are you sure?'

Her lips parted, forming a perfect 'oh', and she stared up at him, so close now, his body locking hers to the wall, so she couldn't think straight, couldn't do anything other than feel. The air between them reverberated with tension and need—she could taste adrenaline in her mouth.

'Or would you like me to kiss you, Mia?'

Her blood screamed in her ears. What was happening? Was this a dream? Why on earth would he be here, offering this? And now? She tried to think straight, tried to put logical thought in front of logical thought, but her mind wouldn't cooperate.

'You can't,' she groaned. Something was pushing its way into the forefront of her brain. Something important she needed to grab hold of. She lifted a hand to his chest, to hold him right where he was, and then she saw it. Her engagement ring.

She was getting married.

Okay, it wasn't a love match either. In fact, she barely knew her husband and had no expectation that he was honouring any kind of old-fashioned celibacy arrangement in the lead-up to their wedding. And she didn't much care. This wasn't to be a normal wedding, nor a normal marriage, and Mia found the idea of that quite thrilling. She was charting her own course, plotting a life for herself—finally—that would best suit her. Without her parents' over-the-top meddling at every turn.

Nonetheless, here at this event, tucked away in a corner of the rooftop, the threat of discovery made her blood curdle.

'*I* can't,' she clarified, infusing her voice with a certainty she didn't feel. 'I'm getting married, Luca. For real this time.'

His eyes bored into hers, something in their depths she couldn't understand.

'But you are not married yet, are you?'

She tried to swallow again, past a throat that was thick and raw.

'I—what do you want?'

'An interesting question. Are you sure you would like the answer?'

She squeezed her eyes shut on a wave of feeling, then shook her head a little. Luca's finger beneath her chin had her tilting her face to his. 'I have a proposition for you.'

Her heart slammed into her throat.

'If I'm honest, I'm still reeling from the last proposition we entered into.'

A quick, cynical smile flooded her and was replaced with warmth. She focused over his shoulder. 'I want you to come home with me.'

The floor seemed to open up and swallow Mia whole. 'What?'

'One night.'

She scanned his face, looking for evidence of a joke, but he wasn't smiling now, and there was such a look of intense hunger in his eyes that she gasped, because it was exactly how he'd looked at her that night, by the car.

Desire was a fever pitch in her bloodstream.

'I can't,' she said, desperate to believe that. Luca was the opposite of what she wanted in every way except one—physical. But he was dangerous. Far too dangerous for Mia, who'd experienced more than enough hurt and humiliation in one lifetime. Now she was all about control. Measured, calm, unemotional control.

'Not even for old time's sake,' he prompted with a softness she hadn't expected. In anyone else, that soft tone might have spoken of uncertainty but in Luca it was dangerous.

'There were no old times,' Mia hissed, furious. 'There was a stupid arrangement and one quick, forgettable moment by a car.'

But for a man like Luca, who was all alpha-male pride, her insult appeared to sail right into its mark. His lips twisted in an approximation of a smile but she saw something else in the depths of his eyes, something darker. 'Forgettable?' He dipped his head forward just as she realised she'd wanted him to, as she'd been goading him to. Oh, what kind of fool was she? 'Let's see if this next kiss is any more memorable then.'

He stared at Mia, challenging her, waiting for her to say or do something, to fight back, but instead, to Mia's shock and despair, anger had her pushing up onto the tips of her toes and seeking his mouth with her own, as if to prove to him how far she'd come in the past year, to show him that she wasn't the same stupid, ignorant girl who'd gone blindly into a marriage arrangement with this man.

But how quickly her control was sapped by the desire that instantly flared between them, as his body pressed hers to the wall, holding her immobile, as he then demanded—and received—her total surrender, the tables utterly turned. The kiss she'd initiated to prove a silly point had become an ultimate surrender.

It had been over a year, and, despite what she'd just said, Mia had never forgotten the power of his mouth. She'd dreamed of this, had longed for it, even when she hated him, and thought him the very worst man on earth. How was it possible that her head and heart could exist in such conflict?

His tongue lashed hers, his body still at first and then moving, a knee moving between her legs then lifting higher, separating her thighs, one arm pressing to the wall at her side, the other curving around her waist, stroking her, holding her, as if he couldn't let her go. But it was all a ruse. A lie. A game.

A game?

Yes. That seemed appropriate. For whatever reason, he'd played Mia. She couldn't understand it, because there had been so much in their arrangement for him to benefit from: the business had seemed so important to him—he'd spent hours with her father, going over the corporate structure, hinting at plans he'd developed to turn Marini Enterprises into a global powerhouse. He'd seemed fully invested, as though buying Marini Enterprises was the most important thing in his world. And then he'd disappeared into thin air.

But these were logical thoughts, and Mia was well beyond the ability to be logical. Her brain was mush, rendered that way by the power of his nearness, the chemistry that sparked between them like a match being struck. She felt its heat and flame ignite inside her body, as though her veins were flooded by pure rocket fuel.

'Luca,' she groaned his name, liked the taste of it, the feel of it, the weight of it against her tongue, the way they rolled together, a tsunami of feelings, but there was terror too, because this was all too much. By the car that night it had been powerful, but like an electrical shock, sharp and succinct, splitting her world in two, then it was over. This was long, growing, a spreading heat that was gripping Mia, changing her, making her want things she couldn't understand, things that were powerful and overwhelming and *necessary*.

She was a woman, damn it. At twenty-three, she was old enough to understand enough about her body and yet she had no experience. While in theory she knew what was going on, the reality of these sensations was totally overwhelming and daunting.

His hand moved to her waist, to the silk shirt she wore, lifting it slightly, just an inch, separating it from the waistband of her full, ballgown skirt so his fingertips brushed her bare skin and she trembled, goosebumps covering her flesh, responding to the possessive glide of his fingers, and all the while a pulse began to beat between her legs, overheating her body. This had to stop, this had to stop, a little voice tried desperately to drag her back to a place of reason, but feelings were drowning it out, the rushing of her blood too loud to allow for any thought.

His fingers crept higher, beneath her shirt, all the way to the underside of her bra, touching her there, as if they were so much more than this. As if he hadn't treated her like dirt. It was too much. Everything was overwhelming to Mia;

she couldn't breathe, and yet she needed to. She needed space. In the midst of passion, she clung to that one fact: he'd treated her—and her parents—so badly, in a way she could never, ever forgive. She hated him, with all her soul. Luca Cavallaro was not a man to be trusted.

With a guttural, soul-destroying cry, she pushed at his chest, anger making her strong, her breath wrenched from her body as she tried to regain her footing, staring at him across air that sparked with a strange, cosmic energy.

What was happening?

Luca showed no emotion. His face was carefully muted of it, but in the depths of his eyes she saw something, *felt* something. Too quickly, he concealed that, too.

'Forgettable?' he prompted, the derision in his voice showing how easy it was to see through her lie. Damn it! She'd tried to hurt his pride, to dent his ego, to prove how much she'd grown, but why bother when he could so easily scatter her resolve?

'Yes,' she spat, anger vibrating through her, the lie one she clung to even when he'd just proved it to be exactly that: a lie. 'You say you've thought about me, Luca? Well, I haven't thought about you at all, except to reflect on how glad I am I didn't end up married to such a heartless bastard!'

Again, his eyes shuttered, hiding something from her, but Mia was too incensed to care. 'How dare you come here and think you can... you can...'

'You kissed me,' he reminded her quietly.

'Yes, but only because you—'

'Because you wanted to,' he interrupted, so close she could feel his breath. 'Don't lie to me again, Mia.'

She frowned. 'When have *I* lied to you?'

His brows shot up with evident surprise. 'I didn't come here to litigate the past.'

'Good, because I have no interest in talking to you.'

He spoke as though she hadn't. 'I am offering you one night, Mia. One night that we should have shared then, that I think we both still want. Our engagement was a mistake, our marriage would have been doomed to fail from the start, but *this*—' he gestured between them '—is undeniable.'

'What the actual hell?' she shouted, spurred to raise her voice by the tide of feelings threatening to engulf her. He pressed a finger to her lips, reminding her where they were, and that they were far from alone.

'Come home with me. Stay the night.'

The words were the most seductive she'd ever

heard, rendered that way by the sexual awareness he'd awoken within her over a year ago.

'Why on earth would I do something as stupid as that, Luca Cavallaro?' She was pleased with the derisive anger in her words, with the way her brain was asserting itself over her libido, even if her voice did shake a little.

'Because you want to,' he prompted, eyes holding hers with the force of a thousand suns. 'As much as I want you to.' His finger lifted to the corner of her lips, brushing her soft flesh. 'Come to me, Mia.'

It made no sense. He was the one who'd walked out on their marriage. 'You left me on our wedding day.'

'And I don't regret that,' he responded sharply.

She glared at him. 'I seriously hate you.'

His eyes narrowed. 'This isn't about hate, or love, or a wedding. It's about one thing, and one thing only. So ask yourself, do you want me enough to forget the past, Mia?'

How on earth could she admit to that? Even when he was right, she hated herself for being willing to ignore the way he'd treated her and go home with him! She clung to defiant anger with difficulty. 'Pigs will fly before I'd ever do anything quite so stupid.'

Their eyes locked and it was a silent, angry war of attrition, a fierce battle. But before she could stalk away, he caught her hand, her wrist, his thumb padding over her flesh. 'We'll see, *cara*.'

And with that, he turned on his heel and disappeared around the corner, his dark head joining the crowd. She watched him until he was absorbed by the milling guests. Mia collapsed into the seat, a maelstrom of feelings and uncertainty.

CHAPTER TWO

MIA DIDN'T GO to him that night. How could she? He'd torn her pride into tatters, but she'd worked hard to rebuild it in the intervening twelve months. She'd rebuilt herself.

Not to mention, she was technically engaged.

Okay, her engagement was definitely not normal. She wasn't in a relationship with Lorenzo and they both understood that. Their marriage would be barely more than a business partnership, only they intended to live together afterwards. Lorenzo was free to see whomever he wished until they were married and he'd made it abundantly clear that he expected her to do the same.

She couldn't hang her resistance on the idea of infidelity—it was so much more complicated.

She was afraid.

Afraid of how much she wanted Luca. Of how she turned to sun-warmed butter in his arms. Of how he made her forget the past: her anger, her hurt, the bitterness of betrayal. Of how easily he made her forget that he was untrustworthy and despicable.

Of how, when she was in his arms, she wasn't capable of rational thought.

But what would happen if she went to his home?

She groaned audibly, in the safety of her bedroom long after the charity event had concluded, staring at her reflection in the floor-to-ceiling mirror her mother had had installed. 'If one can see oneself often, one is less inclined to have the second biscuit, darling.'

Mia was getting married in two months, and she was a virgin. Not by design, but because her parents were strict and protective, and Mia had never been given the freedom to date. Or was there another reason Jennifer had been so controlling in that regard? Any time a man had so much as looked at Mia, Jennifer had been sure to intervene, to tell Mia she was imagining it or that he couldn't be trusted. Mia had taken those messages to heart—was it any wonder she had very little confidence with the opposite sex?

She was getting married with the sole purpose of having children. For her father, it was about the business, for her husband-to-be, it was also about the business, but for Mia, it began and ended with family—the family she had craved since she'd been a little girl and her parents had died, and she'd known the strange no-man's-land of a care home before Gianni and Jennifer had adopted her.

She wanted a family of her own, and Lorenzo could provide that.

But she wasn't an idiot. In order to have children, she'd first need to have sex, and wouldn't it be nice—preferable, anyway—to have some experience before surrendering to her marital bed? Lorenzo left her cold. She didn't desire him at all, and she was pretty sure that was mutual, whereas Luca had the ability to turn her blood to lava with a single look.

Only Luca couldn't be trusted. Not again.

Was there a way to have her cake and eat it too?

Mia stood up straighter, her eyes narrowing, thinking of how much had changed for her in the past twelve months.

Back then, Mia had been vulnerable, too eager to please everyone, so she didn't question, didn't negotiate, didn't do anything except allow herself to be bowled over by desire for Luca. But now? She knew what he was like. She wouldn't be lied to, she wouldn't be hurt, she wouldn't be tricked.

Could she even play him at his own game, and win?

The idea sent sparks of anticipation through her.

What if she were to go to him and take exactly what she wanted, then walk away without a backwards glance, just as he had? What if she were to go to him and *demand* answers for what he'd done? All year, she'd wondered *why*. Over and over, the single word had rattled through her brain, tormenting her, because she couldn't understand how any person could be so evil as to no-show their own wedding.

If she went to him, could she take what she wanted—indulge her desire *and* get the answers she desperately wanted—and emerge unscathed?

Of course you can, a voice from deep in Mia's soul chided, and she wanted to believe that voice, that promise.

Mia's heart began to rush, and her fingers trembled with the possibilities before her.

She would never have chased him down, but having this opportunity laid out before her, wouldn't she be a fool not to take it up? It would be one night, in which he was completely fair game, and then she'd disappear, never seeing him again, the whole matter put to rest behind her, once and for all. Allowing her to marry with a clean slate?

'Argh!' she cried into the room, for surely even contemplating this was madness! And yet she found the idea impossible to dismiss, impossible to let go of. And so, the next night, having said goodnight to her parents and walked up to her bedroom, in the time-honoured tradition of overprotected children everywhere, she silently crept out of her window, climbed down the trellis and walked quickly to the street to wait for a ride-share, adrenaline making her blood roar.

He'd expected her to come.

He'd wanted her.

But it was only when Mia didn't arrive at his home that Luca realised just how much he'd been looking forward to possessing her after all. She'd lit a fire of need in his belly that night by his car, a year ago, and no one else had extinguished it since. It was her innocence, and the vulnerability he sensed within her, that stirred something up in his chest. But those feelings were at odds with his anger towards her and her family for the scam they'd been running.

Innocent? Hardly.

She played the part, but Mia Marini had been all too willing to con him into a billion-dollar hole. Oh, Luca could have afforded it, but that wasn't the point. He was nobody's fool. He'd worked hard and considered at every turn that it was his pride and reputation on the line— the reputation he'd built as a tribute to his late mother, and to make his father eat crow. He wasn't about to buy a worthless company and have the world—his father, particularly—laugh at his stupidity.

Nonetheless, his anger towards Mia now had as much to do with his disappointment that she hadn't arrived at his home as it did with her original betrayal.

His body was alive and waiting, ready, desperately hungry for her. Yet she didn't show up. He cursed her for yet another sin, even as he dreamed of that kiss at the rooftop bar, and craved more, so, so much more.

She passed six churches in the two blocks before reaching his inner-city villa, and, as the car pulled up, she wondered if there'd been a sign there for her to stop, reconsider what she was doing. To go and worship at an actual altar rather than the altar of Luca's physical perfection and the possibility of sexual satisfaction. But Mia was feeling reckless. A storm was brewing, more powerful than any cyclone, and she wouldn't—couldn't—run away from it.

Doubts, however, rolled like thunder through her belly as she stepped out and looked around, awed by the beauty of this street, with ancient cobblestones and beautiful trees, growing lush and green towards the historic façades of these homes. She moved quickly, unwilling to be seen. Sicilia was surprisingly small, and her parents were well known, an old and powerful family. It would be just her luck for some cousin of her father's to see Mia and mention it in passing. It was one of the reasons her gilded cage was so effective. There were not many places Mia could go without meeting someone who knew her parents and would report back. That was just how it worked around here.

And so she had to move quickly; there was no time for regrets.

She took the steps with haste, reached the doorbell and hesitated for the briefest of moments before pressing it, keeping her head bent, lest someone walk past and spot her.

Heart rushing, blood pounding, she stood waiting, nervous, hungry, but not for food: anxiety and tension of the best possible kind were making her body hum and zip.

She pressed the doorbell again, jabbing her finger against it, other emotions beginning to rush through her now, like panic and doubt— but those emotions belonged to the old Mia, to the version of herself she'd been before Luca had, inadvertently, forced her to wake up and start taking control of her life. Before she could act on those unwanted feelings, the big old timber door creaked a little, moved, opened, and Luca was standing on the other side.

He wore suit trousers and a collared shirt with the sleeves pushed up to reveal his tanned forearms. He looked as though he was still working, perhaps. Or maybe entertaining? The thought hadn't even occurred to Mia, but Luca had invited her for the previous night. Perhaps he was busy this evening? Mia considered all of these options in the space of a couple of very fraught seconds, and then the static noise in her brain became overwhelming as her eyes lifted to Luca's and pleasure made every part of her, even her toes, tingle.

'I shouldn't have come,' she murmured, without attempting to leave.

He stared at her for a beat. 'Do you want to go?'

She pressed her teeth into her lower lip, eyes huge in her face, and slowly shook her head.

For a moment, relief flashed in his eyes, then he reached out, a simple gesture, one that Mia had always thought embodied trust, because he was asking her to put her hand in his, to walk with him. It was somehow both simple and far too intimate and yet she needed to get off the street, so she lifted her hand and brushed her fingers against his, trembling at the moment of connection, eyes jerking to his with surprise.

How could a simple glance of flesh be so incendiary? Then again, hadn't it been like this before? Wasn't that part of why she'd been so overwhelmed by the idea of marrying him?

She exhaled a breath of relief when the door closed, glad that she'd crossed the first hurdle, glad that at least she was away from the risk of discovery by someone her parents might know.

She paled at the enormity of this, but then Luca pulled her, through the enormous entrance foyer towards a glass-fronted living room with elegant leather sofas, glass and steel coffee tables and bronze lamps, so the impression was immediately both comfortable and architectural. There was a half-finished glass of something on the coffee table. Whisky? Despite the fact Mia never drank, she disentangled her fingers from his, walked to the glass and took a sip, closing her eyes as the liquid fired courage into her veins.

When she opened her eyes, it was to find Luca staring at her, appraising her, as if weighing her up somehow, working out just what to do with her.

But the whisky had worked, and Mia's courage was returning in spades. This was about her—what she wanted and needed. For far too long she'd been pushed around and manoeuvred to suit other people. She'd been sent away from Sicilia, from the home she loved, from the light she loved, to a cold, dark boarding school in England because it was her mother's wish. She'd come home after making friends and a life in England, because it was her parents' wish. She'd stayed living at home even when she'd found an apartment she could rent, because it was her parents' wish. She'd turned down job offers because her father had insisted she work in the family business—that was her destiny. She'd agreed to marry Luca Cavallaro before she'd even met him, because her parents had convinced her that it was wise and necessary. Her entire life had been a procession of 'yes, yes, yes', from Mia and, just this once, she wanted to take something all for herself, to hell with the consequences.

Besides, there would be no consequences.

Luca Cavallaro wasn't in her life, by his own choosing. He was nothing to her and she was nothing to him, except, perhaps, unfinished business. And if she could exploit that connection, so what?

'Take me to bed, Luca. I don't have all night.'

His eyes sparked with something like surprise, briefly, but then he covered it, his features neutral and impassive, his handsome, symmetrical face captivating and compelling—she couldn't look away.

'What about your fiancé?' he growled, and with good reason: Mia had held Lorenzo up like a shield the last time they'd spoken.

Her eyes met Luca's head-on and she forced herself to be brutally honest, because it was important to her honour that Luca should know she wasn't someone who would ever cheat. 'He's a free agent until we're married, and so am I.'

His eyes narrowed with a speculative power that made her knees knock and he prowled towards her, stopping just short of touching. 'Are you sure?'

'What, have you suddenly developed a conscience, Luca?' she scoffed. 'You're the one who propositioned me.'

He lifted her chin, tilting her face to his. 'I am simply interested.'

'Yes,' she admitted after a beat, the air rushing out of her lungs in a single whoosh. 'I'm sure. We discussed our expectations. We're not a couple and there's no point pretending. As long as we're both discreet, we can do what we want until the wedding.'

It was evidently enough for Luca. He paused only to lift the whisky and take a drink, his eyes holding hers, and she trembled at the intimacy of that too, of sharing a glass with him. His Adam's apple shifted as he swallowed and then he held out the glass to her lips. 'Open.'

Wordlessly, she did exactly that.

He tipped a little more of the alcohol in and then placed the glass on the table, watching as she drank, as a tiny drop of the amber-coloured liquid escaped from the corner of her mouth. An invitation, evidently, because he leaned down and chased it with his tongue, and then captured her lips, tilting her head back with the force of his kiss, his fingers weaving into her pale hair, holding her steady when she might otherwise have slumped to the ground, rendered quite weak by the rush of pleasure.

All doubts fled.

She was doing this.

It was right.

It felt right. And when he lifted her and carried her against his chest, kissing her as he strode through the beautiful apartment, it was just perfect.

She was slimmer than a year ago, those curves that had had the frustrating habit of appearing in his mind at the least convenient times were smaller, but she was still stunning and voluptuous, and so natural. A testament to womanly beauty, from her generous breasts to her tapered-in waist and wide hips, rounded bottom, he wanted to lose himself exploring her valleys and peaks—and he would.

I don't have all night.

Well, nor did he. At least, he didn't have the patience to last the night. But he had now, this moment, and he wanted Mia. Because she could have been his?

Or because she was different from the women he usually dated?

It was strange to want someone you knew to be capable of such a deception, and yet he did want her. This was an aberration for a man famed for his vice-like grip of self-control, but it was just one night. Then he'd never think of her again.

As if to underscore to himself the purely physical nature of this, he placed her on the ground just inside his bedroom and began to remove her clothing, piece by piece, not slowly, not even particularly sensually, more as if he needed to see her naked and tick that box. His fantasies had been filled with what he'd *imagined* she looked like, surely the reality would be disappointing.

He stripped away her cotton shirt and simple bra, revealing her breasts, pale with dusky pink tips, better than he'd fantasised about. His gut tightened. Her arms were slim, tanned, her decolletage delicate and fascinating, with a pulse point that was rushing beneath his languid inspection. She stood perfectly still, eyes wide, as if she hadn't expected this, as if she hadn't come here for it.

Perhaps she'd thought it would be different. More foreplay. More touching. But hell, Luca wanted Mia *now*. Keeping a grip, barely, he moved his hands down her waist, squeezing at her hips a little before sliding down her skirt. It was elasticated at the waist and went easily. She stood in just a scrap of cotton. He wanted to kneel before her and reverently remove it, but he was still angry with her for the lie of a year ago, and even angrier because he wanted her despite her betrayal. What kind of fool did that make him?

Her breath snagged as he slid his fingers into the elastic of her underpants and began to push them lower, so he felt it against his forehead, warm and sweet smelling.

She stepped out of her underpants and kicked off her shoes, losing a vital inch in height, so he towered over her. He hadn't noticed how dramatic their height difference was before—then again, she'd only ever worn shoes around him, and always heels. Was she self-conscious about her petite stature?

She was delightfully short and curved, the stuff men dreamed about, so womanly and soft, her skin like rose petals.

'Please stop,' she whispered, so Luca's chest

thudded. Stop? Now? His eyes jerked to hers, searching.

'You're staring at me,' she explained, gesturing to her body.

'Yes.'

Her cheeks flooded with pink. 'I—don't like to be looked at.'

He frowned, wondering at her meaning.

'Would you prefer I touch, *cara*?'

She trembled, her nipples growing taut, her body swaying a little, so he took her physical response as confirmation, moving closer, close enough to feel her warmth, before wrapping his arm around her waist and drawing her forward, hard against his body, so he could indeed touch her, all of her, from the sweet curves of her bottom to the beautiful roundness of her breasts. He cupped her rear, pressing her against him, his arousal hard through the inconvenient barrier of his own clothing. She made a muffled groaning noise, tilting her head back, giving him access to the swan-like neck, so graceful, and he took full advantage, pressing his lips to her pulse point first, flicking it with his tongue before suckling, taking pleasure in the idea of her getting a mark from his ministrations, hoping to leave an imprint on her flesh of where she'd been—and what she'd been doing.

Her responsiveness was his undoing. He

moved his mouth to hers and she writhed against him, just like that night near the car, so desperate and hungry and he couldn't resist touching her all over now, moving one hand to her breast, cupping it, fondling it, feeling the weight in his hand until he was taut with need, then driving it lower, over the swell of her hip, between her legs, parting her thighs and finding her womanhood, her warm, sweet, feminine core and pressing a finger inside, her moist, slick heat breaking the last of his self-control, so he kissed her as he undressed himself, so hungry and desperate for her, so overcome with needs that he barely had time to grab protection—an essential for Luca, who never intended to have children, and particularly not accidentally. Having lived with the consequences of being an unwanted child himself, he had no intention of inflicting that pain on another living soul.

His arousal was so tight it hurt to extend the rubber over his length; it hurt even more because it required him moving away from Mia to his bedside table, and taking a few seconds to perform the miraculous act. But once sheathed, he spun back to her, wild, like a caged animal with a glimpse of escape, and all the emotions this woman brought out in him rode to the fore. Anger. Frustration. Betrayal. Need.

'Come here,' he barked, the words short because he couldn't help but resent the effect she had on him.

Her eyes widened, her tongue darted out and she moved, unsteadily, across to him, her body so beautifully perfect, he couldn't tear his eyes off her as she sat down on the edge of the bed and stared at him, lips parted and breasts heaving with each rushed breath.

He prowled towards Mia, intentional and determined, standing above her, naked, hard, ready, eyes finding hers, cynicism unknowingly written across his face as he brought himself down, one hand on either side of her head, pressed to the bed, his body over hers.

'I am glad you decided to come to me,' he admitted gruffly.

She didn't say anything. Her eyes were huge in her face, beautiful and mesmerising and awash with feelings he couldn't decipher and didn't want to know about. He couldn't allow himself to care about Mia. It was bad enough that her body had haunted his thoughts without his consent for this long year, but he wouldn't allow her humanity to seep into him. Better to stick to the bare facts of who she was, and all the reasons he couldn't trust her.

But that didn't mean they couldn't enjoy each other's bodies.

He didn't want to think about the betrayal of

her parents now. He nudged her thighs apart with his knee, wishing he wanted her less so he could play with her more, but instead, he held himself over her, contenting himself with watching her face as he drove into her, hard and fast, he was filled with urgency, then still, because she froze, and he realised that the tightness around his length spoke of absolute inexperience, that the woman beneath him, around him, was a virgin.

His usually sharp mind could barely make sense of it.

Mia Marini had been going to marry him.

And she was a virgin.

He couldn't say why but those two statements felt incongruent. He pushed up, staring at her, looking for answers in her face, but she was already recovering, moving her hips, drawing him deeper, and, while questions were launching through his mind, he was still driven by his body's needs, by urges that made it impossible to see clearly through the forest. Thankfully, he knew enough to pause, to demand, roughly, 'Are you okay?'

She nodded, quickly. 'Oh, yes,' she groaned, twisting beneath him, her muscles squeezing his length, so he pushed aside chivalric duty and any concerns of decency and focused on what she'd come here for. There'd be time to interrogate and analyse. Later.

Pushing back up to watch her properly, he moved gently, slowly, then he gave up on studying her because he needed to kiss her, to taste her, his mouth hungrily seeking hers, his tongue emulating his body's rhythms, his hands greedily running over her, finding her breasts, weighing them, running fingers across her nipples until she was crying out, exploding, her orgasm sharp and explosive, almost robbing him of his own control, but Luca refused to finish yet, refused for this to be over. He waited—barely—for her to come back to earth, for her breathing to slow, and then he was moving again, faster and harder this time, the sound of their flesh slapping together driving him almost over the edge, so he gritted his teeth, waited, watched, listened for Mia's own cries to grow sharp and desperate and only then did he let go of his control and join her in the sublime ecstasy of post-orgasm euphoria.

He rolled off Mia, onto his back, staring at the ceiling, taking a second to regain his wits, trying to order his thoughts, but her breathing was so rushed, her body so close, that it was impossible. He needed proper space from her. He needed to move away from her fragrance, her nearness, from the temptation to reach out and touch her.

'Give me a moment,' he muttered, standing, prowling from his room and into the adjoining bathroom, bracing his palms on the edge of the sink, staring at his reflection, waiting for the world to start making sense again.

Luca was very rarely surprised.

He generally considered himself to be a good judge of people, and yet he hadn't expected this. He'd thought Mia's quivering innocence to be an act. He'd thought her a very, very good liar.

Because when she'd kissed him, out by the car, her body had instinctively responded to his—she hadn't seemed like a virgin then. She'd been a siren, calling to him, inviting him, begging him…and he'd wanted to listen. He'd been so angry that night. So angry with her, her parents, for the discovery his team had just informed him of. If he'd slept with her then, it would have been to punish her, and, while Luca knew he had a dark side, he wasn't, he hoped, quite so messed up to resort to using sex for anything other than giving and taking pleasure…

He bit back a curse, because whatever tonight had been, it had gone in a different direction from what he'd anticipated.

He took his time. He needed to. Removing

and disposing of the condom, he then had a quick shower, hoping the water would bring clarity, so he could go back out there and calmly ask Mia just what the hell she was thinking not to at least *tell him* that she'd never been with a man before.

But much to Luca's disgust, whenever he contemplated that, all he could focus on was the fact that he was her first, and a primal, ancient thrill made him grow hard again.

It was ten long, disjointed minutes before Luca felt he could join Mia, and when he stalked into his room, he did so with a command: 'Okay, Mia Marini, explain yourself, right now.'

But there was no answer, because there was no Mia. She'd disappeared into thin air.

'G'day.'

Max Stone's broad Australian accent boomed down the phone line. Luca, in a foul temper, furrowed his brow. He could practically hear the sunshine and salt water in Max's tone, and imagined him somewhere near one of their pearl farms, happy, relaxed, the exact opposite of how Luca was feeling.

'Max. What's up?'

'Just checking in. Did you have a look at the prospectus I sent you?'

Luca ground his teeth. His father had been

trying to get Luca interested in the Stone family business for years—he took a direct approach and Luca enjoyed giving a direct answer: no. But Max was more skilled. He waved things beneath Luca's nose that would be almost impossible to ignore.

'I glanced at it,' Luca lied. The figures for opening a new flagship Stone store in Tulsa were persuasive, and Max knew it as well as Luca. What Max was really asking was for Luca to weigh in on some of the trickier decisions, such as location and size.

These were matters Luca had no intention of discussing, even though he'd immediately formed some thoughts.

'And?'

He dragged a hand through his hair. 'And, to be completely honest, the Stone stores are the last things on my mind right now.'

Silence crackled, and Luca grimaced, because he'd made an uncharacteristic error. When talking with Max, he had to keep his wits about him—his brother was too insightful and could read Luca like a book. If Luca even got close to intimating that he'd been obsessively thinking about the woman he slept with last night, Max would push for more details and before Luca knew it he'd be revealing that he'd seduced the woman he'd been supposed to marry a year ago.

It wasn't as if he kept secrets from Max. He'd never needed to. But the whole business with the Marini family was something Luca didn't want to discuss.

And he definitely didn't see the need to go into last night.

Luca was a man who liked to be in control, and things with Mia had spiralled way, way out of his comfort zone. She was different from what he'd expected, and her virginity had caught him totally off guard. So too her disappearing act.

With a tightening of his jaw, he stared straight ahead, eyes sweeping the view without really seeing it.

'Come on. I'd love your input.'

Luca let out a harsh laugh. 'You'd love me to sign my life away on the bottom line.'

'Don't be so dramatic.' Luca could hear his brother's grin. 'Besides, would it really be so bad to join the family business?'

Luca gripped his phone tighter, that simple, throwaway phrase one Max used without thinking, without any idea how it goaded Luca.

'It's your family business, not mine.'

'You don't like him, you don't respect him, but, however you may *feel* about the man, Carrick Stone *is* your father, we are your family.'

'Yes. You are.' Luca ground his teeth. 'But

that doesn't mean I have any interest in working for him.'

'With him, Luc. Not for him. You'd be equal to me, to him.'

'Does it occur to you that I cannot be equal to him? That I cannot—it's too much.' Luca sighed heavily. 'You know why I feel this way.'

Max was quiet a moment longer. After all, he did know. He'd been there when Luca had arrived at their home in Sydney, grieving the sudden death of his mother, reeling from the discovery of his famous, wealthy father, simmering with resentments at having been ignored and unwanted. Then, there'd been the sense of competitiveness Carrick Stone had tried to instil in both boys, an almost gladiatorial fight for supremacy that, thankfully, they'd both grown out of. Luca and Max both had a lot of reasons to despise their father.

Max sighed heavily. 'I get it, Luca. Carrick is—you know we're on the same page about his lifestyle, his decisions, his attitudes.'

Luca closed his eyes. His father had treated women like dirt, and his own mother had paid the ultimate price, because she'd fallen in love with him and been destroyed by that love. Carrick had lived and left a trail of destruction in his wake because he'd never really loved or cared for anyone—even his sons. He was the lowest of the low.

'But almost for as long as I've known you, I've thought it would be great to do this together. You hated coming to live with us, but, for me, I suddenly wasn't alone. I had a brother, and someone to do all this with.'

For the second time in twenty-four hours, Luca felt a pang of regret. He'd walked out on Carrick as soon as he could, but he'd also walked out on Max. Was he being selfish, just like Carrick, to avoid his responsibilities to the family business? None of this was Max's fault…

'I'll look at the prospectus again,' Luca conceded with a grimace. After all, that wasn't too much to ask. 'And send you an email with my thoughts.'

Luca disconnected the call with a sense of misgiving, but whatever headspace he had to think about his father's business evaporated pretty quickly. He closed his eyes and there she was: Mia Marini, taking up all his thoughts, driving him crazy even when she was nowhere to be seen, and Luca had the unpleasant realisation that he'd been utterly and completely wrong: one night hadn't been enough. He wanted more, he wanted answers, he wanted Mia.

CHAPTER THREE

ALL MIA COULD think of as she stared at her reflection in the large mirrors of the bridal shop was that it was next-level inappropriate to be trying on a wedding gown the day after having sex with someone other than your fiancé. It didn't matter how many times she told herself that it wasn't cheating, that she and Lorenzo had no expectations of their relationship being anything like a normal marriage, it still felt the complete opposite of the fairy tale Mia had, at one point, desperately hoped for.

Well, if she wasn't to have the fairy-tale marriage, at least this time her dress wasn't going to be such a disaster.

She'd deliberately chosen something that was dramatically different to before. Not a hint of lace or tulle, the gown was instead simple and elegant. Cream silk, cut on the bias, the dress somehow flattered the curves Mia liked and played down those that she didn't. Her mother would hate it; Mia didn't care. She'd seen the image of herself covered in ice cream, staring at the sky, so many times: she never wanted to wear a puffy, tulle dress ever again.

The fact this was close to white was a miracle.

If she had her way, though, Mia would elope. There'd be no wedding, as such. Just a signing of the certificate, to mark the fact the wedding was, essentially, a business deal.

'All okay, *signorina*?'

Mia's body felt different. How could people look at her and not see how she'd spent the night? Heat coloured her cheeks as she remembered the way it had felt to have Luca drive into her, so strong and hard, to have her mind blown with pleasure again and again.

'Fine.' She nodded quickly, her voice hoarse. 'I like it.'

'I will trim the hem to this length, to allow for the heels you showed me.'

'Great.' Mia smiled over-brightly. She didn't want to think about Luca again.

She'd done what she'd set out to do. She'd lost her virginity, gained experience and walked out on him while his back was turned. Okay, it wasn't anywhere near as hurtful as what he'd done to her—ditching her on her wedding day—but there'd been a petty sense of satisfaction in disappearing from his home while he showered.

Then again, he'd probably been glad.

As for Mia, she'd wished, the whole drive home, that she hadn't left, and not just because she'd also intended to get answers from him, to find out why he'd ditched her on their wedding day. But mostly, she'd wished, more than anything, that she was back in that bed with Luca: naked, strong, powerful, skilled, showing her all the things her body could feel, teaching her about sex, mastering her so cleverly, as he'd already done.

Instead, she'd quickly dressed and slipped out of the front door, onto the quiet midnight streets, and disappeared into the dark—and from his life, for good.

She emerged from the bridal store distracted, head dipped, so at first she didn't notice the shiny grey car with jet-black tinted windows parked in a no standing zone outside the shop. But when a car drove past and beeped at the offending vehicle, Mia looked up and did a double take.

Luca.

Here.

The coincidence was uncanny. But *of course* it wasn't a coincidence. He was waiting for her.

With a heart that wouldn't stop jolting, she

changed course, moving towards him as if drawn by magnetic force, stopping a metre away, staring. Her insides leapt, the recognition overwhelming. 'What are you doing here?' Had she forgotten something? She did a quick mental catalogue of what she'd taken to his house—purse, phone, keys. She definitely had all those. Something else? 'How did you know where I was?'

His eyes flashed to hers. 'Get in the car, Mia.' The command made her pulse shiver.

'Thank you for the kind invitation, but I think I'll choose to decline.'

He ground his teeth, his jaw visibly moving with the effort. 'Get. In.'

'It is a free country, isn't it? Or are you proposing to kidnap me?'

'If that's what it takes.' He moved closer, and a thrill of anticipation rushed through her. Mia knew she should have been annoyed at his heavy-handed, dictatorial manner but, in truth, she found it exciting. The thought of being kidnapped by Luca conjured all sorts of strange, unacknowledged fantasies. Mia remembered how it had felt to be carried by him last night, as though she weighed little more than a feather. She wanted to feel that again. Her determination was slipping.

Looking in one direction and then the other,

she jerked her attention back to Luca. 'Only because I don't want anyone my parents or fiancé know to see me talking to you. Of all people!' She was pleased at how withering her voice sounded.

'Heaven forbid.' His own was scathing. 'Now.' He wrenched open the door and gestured impatiently for her to take her seat.

Mia shot him one last fulminating glare then moved to the car, careful to give him a wide berth. It was a futile manoeuvre, because if she'd hoped to avoid being close to him, inhaling his intoxicating fragrance, she was just about to step into the lion's den. The moment she was inside the car, sliding across the plush back seat to the far side, he joined her, folding his far larger frame into the seat then leaning forward and pressing a button that lowered the screen between himself and the driver.

'Leave us. I'll call when I'm ready.'

'Yes, sir.'

The driver left and then Luca turned to Mia, eyes swirling with dark emotions. 'What happened last night?'

She blinked at him, deliberately avoiding the question. 'You need me to explain it to you? I would have thought you understood the biology...'

His expression showed he wasn't amused. 'You disappeared.'

She tucked her hands together on her lap. 'No, I left after we finished.'

His eyes probed hers, as if looking for something, she didn't know what.

'And you think that's okay?'

She stared at him, genuinely dumbfounded. 'I'm sorry, what?'

'You left without even having a conversation with me? Without explaining your virginity? Without telling me—anything?'

Anger was a whip, stirring Mia to a fever pitch. 'Isn't that a little like the pot calling the kettle black?' she demanded fiercely. 'You left me standing in a church in a ridiculous wedding dress with three hundred people watching! You seriously think *I* owe *you* an explanation?'

'So what does that mean?' he snapped. 'That last night was payback?'

'Is that your way of saying sex with me was a punishment? Gee, thanks,' she muttered, reaching for the door.

His hand came across, grabbing her wrist, and sparks ignited beneath her skin.

'You know that's not what I meant.' His voice was a sensual rumble, and he was closer now, his body framing hers, big and strong. She shrank back into the seat, afraid of how her desires might overtake everything else.

'Yeah, well, I don't care. You can think whatever the hell you want. It happened. We had sex. Isn't that why you invited me over?'

'Yes.' His answer came without delay and Mia tried to ignore the strange sinking feeling in her chest cavity. 'But I didn't realise you were totally inexperienced.'

Mia glared at him. 'Does it make a difference?'

His frown was instinctive. 'Yes,' he said after a beat. 'You should have mentioned it.'

'And you should have mentioned that you weren't planning to marry me.'

He moved closer, his body magnetic and strong. She licked her lower lip. 'Do you really want to open that Pandora's box, *cara*?' He drawled the term of endearment with a hint of cynicism, so she shivered, despite the attraction sparking in the atmosphere.

'What's that supposed to mean?'

'You were not honest with me either.'

About being a virgin? Why should she have mentioned that? 'It would have come up,' she said with a shake of her head. 'After our wedding.'

'By then, it would have been too late. But you

didn't care. You didn't care that every part of our marriage deal was based on a lie.'

'I—' She couldn't unravel what he was saying. Was her virginity really such a big deal? Big enough for him to say everything else was a lie, too? 'I never lied to you,' she denied.

'Selective truth telling,' he corrected with obvious disgust. 'It is just as bad.'

She frowned. Really? 'I would have thought someone with your experience would have been able to tell…'

'Yes, I could,' he agreed after a dangerous, silky beat. 'Which is why I decided not to marry you, in the end. Why I decided to walk away from you and your family. It was the right decision.'

She flinched, the harshness of his decree cutting her to the bone.

'Fine, good to know,' Mia responded when she could trust herself to speak. 'If you're done, I would like to get on with my day.'

'We're not finished,' he responded, so close the words seemed to reverberate inside her.

'We are *so* finished,' she corrected, lifting a hand to push him away, but he pressed his own over the top, holding it there, his eyes widening as he moved his head closer. 'We're finished,' she repeated, more feebly. 'We were finished the day you left me in that church.' To her frustration, her voice wobbled and she felt the awful sting of tears in the back of her throat, threatening to moisten her eyes. 'I hate you.'

'Not last night,' he reminded her, moving his other hand to her thigh, then lower, to the hem of her dress.

'Yes, I hated you, even last night.'

'So it was revenge. To sleep with me and then run away?'

Heat coloured her cheeks, but whatever she was about to say scattered from her mind as his fingers slid up her inner thigh, towards her sex.

'Did it feel good, Mia? Did you have enough revenge?' He moved his mouth to hers, brushed it lightly then pulled away, so he could look into her eyes. 'Or do you need to punish me some more?'

Say no. Leave. Get out of his car. This man is quicksand and you're falling, falling into a danger you have no skill to navigate.

'I hate you,' was all she said, and she really, really did, but oh, how she wanted him.

His eyes narrowed. 'But do you blame me, Mia? Do you really blame me for not going through with our wedding?'

Her heart dropped to her toes. Hurt lashed her. She knew she couldn't hold a candle to the women he usually dated, she knew she wasn't a show-stopping beauty, or slim like her mother, or confident and worldly, but she had qualities that people might consider more than made up for those shortcomings. She didn't need him to hit her over the head with his lucky escape from marriage to a wallflower like Mia.

'Then why proposition me?' she asked quietly, her desire and anger evaporating in a wave of shock, because his words had been so hurtful.

'Why do you think?' he asked, and then his hand moved higher, all the way to the fabric of her underpants, which he slid aside, his fingers brushing her most sensitive cluster of nerves until she bucked against the back seat of the car, and then he was kissing her, swallowing the groans she offered up to the heavens, losing herself in this moment even when she knew she should tell him to go to hell. It was somehow much more tempting for Mia to be carried to heaven, anyway.

She didn't know what game he was playing— but surely it was a game. She was a toy to him, and he was deriving some kind of pleasure from the push and pull of this, whereas Mia felt as though she were blindly navigating an awful storm.

'Come home with me…again,' he said against the side of her mouth.

Mia had enough wits about her to shake her

head, somewhat unconvincingly. 'No way. Never.'

'Careful, Mia. There's nothing I like more than a challenge.'

His words barely penetrated the thick fog of her brain, and any hope she had of thinking rationally evaporated when he lifted her easily and settled her on his lap, kissing her as he fumbled to push up her skirt and unbutton his trousers so his arousal was shielded only by the flimsy cotton of his boxers. He pushed himself against her sex, and desire exploded through her. Mia rocked on her haunches, wanting, desperate to feel him, as he kissed her and felt her breasts in his palms, delighting in the different sensations that were changing her body chemistry completely.

'Do you still hate me?' he asked with a mocking smile.

'Yes,' she whimpered as he reached around into his back pocket.

'But you want me anyway?' he prompted, and she moaned, because she hated herself for feeling that way, and hated him even more for making her admit it.

She bit down on her lip as he removed his arousal and curved his palm around the base; all she could do was stare, marvel, hunger.

'Say that you want me,' he demanded, the

words harsh, hissed from between his teeth. With the effort of self-control.

'Screw you,' she muttered, those stinging tears forming on her lashes.

He arched a brow, then slid the condom into place. 'That can be arranged.'

It was Mia who moved, sinking down over his length, tilting her back, crying out into the limousine at this new sense of fullness, of perfect, heart-stopping completion. The relief was terrifying.

She rocked up and down, moving as she needed to, pleasure building, waves speeding up, growing in intensity, until she lifted her hands and pressed them to the top of the car, arched fully, so his mouth came down on her breast through the fabric of her shirt and sucked, then bit her nipple lightly, then sucked some more, so all she wanted was to be completely naked.

'Luca,' she groaned as pleasure built to a fever pitch. 'Please.'

Luca took over, gripping her bottom and moving her up and down his length, thrusting his hips off the seat, so powerful and commanding, so demanding. Mia called his name into the air. She was everywhere in the world all at once, a thousand fragments of herself scattered on the wind. She wasn't sure she'd ever be able to go back together again—not in the same way.

He was playing a dangerous game. Dangerous because he no longer understood the rules, he knew only that having sex with Mia was the most compelling and addictive experience he'd had in a long time. Luca had been bored for years. Even his business successes were less exhilarating these days, because there was no longer the risk. He was too talented at what he did.

But with Mia, there was a charge of something that made adrenaline flood his body and he wasn't capable of thinking and planning, he simply acted on instinct. And every instinct had been shouting at him, since he'd emerged to find her gone last night, to finish what they'd started.

But he still wasn't finished, even as his own orgasm receded, and the world began to make sense again.

This wouldn't be their last time together. He wouldn't allow that. He refused to question his motives. He didn't want to analyse why he felt this sudden need to possess the woman he'd turned his back on without regret a year earlier. Was it simply because she was about to marry another man, and some primal jealousy had reared its head? Yet he'd had other lovers who'd married, and it had never bothered Luca.

Not an ounce. So maybe it all came down to un-finished business. To the fact he'd wanted Mia that night, and he'd never had her. To the fact they'd been engaged, both intending to marry when they'd made that arrangement, and yet they hadn't. Their story deserved some comple-tion. Was that it?

Mia, perhaps, did not agree.

She shifted, not meeting his eyes, lifting up from him and moving to the far side of the car, with a surprising amount of grace given the space constraints.

He could sense her prevarication, her doubts returning, so he did the only thing he could and pulled his phone from his pocket, firing off a quick text to his driver.

'That shouldn't have happened,' Mia said, anger directed towards herself. 'Damn you, Luca. You can't just approach me on the street—' A frown changed her features, pull-ing him back in, fascinating him all over again. He'd thought her beautiful last year—distract-ingly so—but he'd fought hard to keep his focus where it had belonged: on the business. Until that kiss, when he'd no longer been able to ig-nore the searing attraction he felt towards her, but by that point, he was already filled with so much anger about her family's lies, he hadn't been able to act on desire.

He looked at Mia now and saw so many different emotions flitting through her expressive eyes. They told a thousand stories; he could see how easy it would be to become enthralled by those eyes, and, much like the king in Scheherazade's tale, to sit and listen each night, waiting for more.

Luca would never be so stupid, of course.

He knew what Mia was capable of, what her parents had embroiled her in.

'Do you have any idea what this wedding means to me?'

'I know what it means to your parents,' he responded swiftly.

She narrowed her eyes. 'To *me*.' She pressed her fingers between her full, rounded breasts.

His eyes dropped and held. He couldn't look away. He was acting like some inexperienced teenager.

Pull yourself together.

'I need to marry him. Anyone could have seen us just now, could have been waiting…this can't keep happening.'

'Why do you need to marry him?' he demanded, curiosity warring with some other, sharper emotion. 'Can you really be so mercenary as to commit yourself to a man you don't know for the sake of your family's business?'

The driver's door closed and Mia startled, annoyed. But before she could put two and two together, the engine had started and the car pulled out into traffic, the screen between driver and passengers going up as the car moved.

'Wait! What's happening?'

'We're driving, Mia, what did you think?'

She gripped the car door. 'No way. Let me out.'

'Answer my question,' he demanded bullishly. 'Why are you so determined to marry him?'

Her features took on a mutinous set as she glared first at him and then beyond him, through the heavily tinted windows. 'Where are we going?'

'Why did you agree to marry me?' he pushed.

Her eyes flew back to Luca's then she turned away from him completely, crossing her arms and staring out of the window. Without answering.

Despite the dark emotions that were threatening to undo his self-control, Luca felt a strange lick of amusement—and a double dose of admiration—for the tactic. But she was seriously underestimating him if she thought he'd let it go.

'Are you so desperate to help your parents, Mia?' A thought occurred to him, one he didn't like but needed to test. 'Or was the whole thing your idea?'

'What are you talking about?' she demanded

hotly, turning back to face him and puffing out a breath to move a pale clutch of silk hair that had drifted in front of her lips. It danced an inch off her face then fell down again. He reached for it, his fingers gentle, guiding it behind her ear and lingering there. Their eyes held, hers troubled, confused, his own, he hoped, devoid of any telltale emotion.

'Your being included to sweeten the deal,' he said darkly. 'Did you volunteer yourself? Or did your parents suggest it?'

Her lips formed a perfect, voluptuous circle. He dug his fingers into the leather seat to stave off the temptation to kiss her again—because a kiss would lead to more and they needed to talk.

'I don't think my inclusion was intended as an inducement,' she said after a beat, her lips pulling to one side, a troubled expression on her face as she once again turned away from him. He hated that. Her many-storied eyes were his to read. Or he wanted them to be.

'Then why?'

But Mia didn't want to have this conversation. 'Tell your driver to let me out.'

'No.'

She shook her head angrily. 'Are you actually intending to kidnap me?'

The decision was instant. 'Yes.'

That got her attention. She pivoted to face

him, chest moving with the force of her breathing. 'Luca Cavallaro, you stop the car this damned minute. Or else I'll—I'll—'

He waited with the appearance of calm when, inside, something was ticking faster than was healthy, making him question the wisdom of this on so many levels.

'You'll...?' he prompted, when silence fell. Her expression was mutinous.

'I haven't made up my mind yet.'

'Well, you have over an hour to think about it. Let me know what my punishment will be.' He leaned closer, deliberately provoking her. 'I like your style of punishment, Mia. Please, do keep it coming.'

CHAPTER FOUR

As a girl, Mia had visited San Vito Lo Capo on vacations. Jennifer had loved the crystal-clear ocean and white sandy beaches, the extra-salty water making for buoyant swimming. They'd always brought a yacht around, and Mia had jumped off the edge, knees bundled to her chest, feeling sublimely contented until pre-adolescence, when Jennifer had begun to make comments about Mia's bikini not being appropriate given Mia's size, or pinching Mia's hips and remarking that Mia should really try the watermelon diet Jennifer was a die-hard fan of.

Somehow, it had soured the beachside town for Mia. She'd started to loathe their trips here and, eventually, managed to get out of coming altogether. So while she could appreciate the beauty of the coastline as Luca's car swept around the corner and produced a breathtaking view of the sea, she couldn't look at this familiar aspect without a curdling sense of anxiety gripping her.

'Tell me we're not stopping here.'

'You do not like it?' he prompted, gesturing to the stunning aquamarine sea.

She clamped her lips together, angled her face away and harumphed.

On the drive from Palermo to the coast, she'd made a thousand resolutions to deal with his apparent kidnapping. One of them was to stop making conversation with him as though they had anything in common.

As though she'd forgiven and forgotten what he'd done to her—the embarrassment and shame his rejection had caused. Last night hadn't been about forgiveness, it had been about...closure. Revenge? Or at least taking back the narrative, taking control, because in the last year, she'd learned the importance of asserting herself, and she wasn't going to forget those lessons.

Luca's laugh was so quiet it was almost inaudible but to Mia, whose nerves were stretched tight, it not only reached her ears but seemed to wrap around her, so she ground her teeth together, wishing there were some way she could inoculate herself against his masculine charms. Hating him apparently wasn't going to cut it.

'Relax, Mia. It's just one night. Perhaps two.'

'Two?' Disbelief rang through the word. 'I

can't stay with you for two nights. Listen to me, Luca, my parents will have kittens if I'm not home after work.'

'Your parents will survive.'

She narrowed her gaze, connecting the dots. 'Did you kidnap me…to hurt them?' She frowned. It didn't make sense. It was Luca who'd let her family down. Her parents were the ones who had every right to be angry, not the other way around.

'Why do you hate us so much, Luca?'

He scanned her face, as if trying to comprehend something, then leaned forward. 'I cannot tell if this is an act, or real.'

'What?'

He reached out, smudging his thumb over her lower lip. As if he could wipe away whatever was making it difficult to read her and see more clearly.

'You don't think I have a right to despise them? And even you, a little, Mia? Perhaps you, most of all.'

Her heart twisted.

'You were willing to go further than either of them.'

'I don't know what you're talking about.'

'You were willing to sell yourself, and your virginity, to the highest bidder, to cover up their scam. How exactly should I feel about you?'

She flinched, his words making absolutely no

sense. Scam? Her parents had a lot of faults, but they were hardly grifters. 'You're delusional.'

He moved closer, eyes flecked with brown and caramel. 'Did you really think I wouldn't find out?'

'Find out what?' she asked with urgency. She needed to understand what he was accusing them of, even when she knew it couldn't be true.

'Perhaps another buyer might not, but I am always cautious when I invest. Did you think our marriage would be enough of an inducement to make me look the other way?'

'Please stop talking in riddles,' she demanded haltingly, 'and tell me what you're accusing us of.'

He was very quiet, and the engine idled, then cut altogether. A moment later, Pietro, Luca's driver, was at the door, opening Luca's side. He immediately resented the intrusion but concealed that from his long-time staffer.

Luca took the briefest possible moment to give some instructions to Pietro then came around to Mia's side, opening the car door and waiting for her to step out. She glared up at him, heart pounding, tempted to refuse to move, but she had no doubt he'd simply reach down and lift her from the car—which had every possibility of leading to the kind of passion they'd just shared. Fighting made them spark.

Something about them was instantly combustible.

Or, maybe sex was always like this? She hoped so.

Because, no matter what was happening between her and Luca, she had no intention of walking away from her engagement, and her marriage. Her heart gave a painful lurch, because she needed to remember what was fantasy and what was real—and nothing about Luca was real. This was a dangerous game they were playing, dangerous because there were no rules and no clear path to victory for either of them.

Despite her misgivings about this place, she couldn't help but admire the villa at which they'd arrived. A wide gravel drive led to a turning circle with a pale yellow fountain at its centre. Four ancient statues of robe-draped women formed an elegant pyramid that led to a dolphin spouting water over their breasts and down into the water below. The sound was beautiful and relaxing. The driveway was surrounded on one side by a grove of citrus trees, fragrant with blossoms at this time of year, and on the other by a garden that might have been quite formal at one time but that was now delightfully overgrown. Wisteria ran rampant over the arbour, and half of the house, and a stone bench seat was covered in lichen and ivy.

The air hummed with bees and the smell of sweet flowers.

She hardened her heart. Against the beauty, and the seductive temptation of this.

The doors to the villa had ornate brass hinges, very old, she guessed, and the doors themselves were wide, timber and painted a lovely turquoise colour that perfectly complemented the glistening ocean beyond the house. The sound of the gently lapping waves called to Mia, but she heard her mother's voice, as clear as a bell, and knew she wouldn't indulge her childish desire to sprint down to the hot sand and into the refreshing ocean.

'You have to take me home,' she said, moving to Luca and pulling on his sleeve.

'Why?' he demanded, looking completely untouchable. In fact, it was impossible to recognise the passionate man she'd just made love to with the determined glittering in his dark eyes. 'So your parents can raffle you off to the next highest bidder? So you can simper and smile across the table, all wide-eyed innocence, for your next target?'

'Stop saying that,' she shouted with rich anger. 'You have no right to speak to me so disdainfully. I entered into our engagement in good faith.' Her hand lifted, finger jabbing his chest. 'You're the one who broke the deal. You're the one who left me...who left me...' Emotions welled inside her. This place had haunted her and was taunting her now, flooding her with memories that weakened her. 'Who left me on our wedding day,' she finished anticlimactically, staring at a point past his shoulder. 'How dare you try to pin any blame on me?'

'On you? Who would have had me sink a billion dollars into a worthless company? Who thought a single kiss might tempt me to ignore common sense and go ahead with the deal anyway?'

She shook her head, to dispel his words, the implication buried in them. She knew the value of their family business because she worked in it—and what was more, she'd seen her parents' lifestyle first-hand for years. 'A worthless company?' She rolled her eyes, hoping her derision would dismiss the very idea from his head.

'You are very beautiful, Mia, and I'm not going to say I wasn't tempted, but I am not stupid enough to gamble my fortune on a woman, no matter how nicely she kisses.'

Mia's fingers tingled with a need to slap him but that would be far too demure. Instead, she shoved him hard in the chest, hard enough to fell someone else, but Luca stood perfectly still, head tilted down at her, almost as if he'd been expecting it. But that wasn't it: it was simply that Luca was always poised for a fight.

'This is all—lies,' she said, pushing him again. 'To what end? Perhaps to assuage your guilty conscience?'

'I have no guilt, Mia.' His calm voice only aggravated her further.

'No guilt,' she repeated, dropping her hands to her sides and staring at him with disbelief. 'You handed me, without a doubt, the worst day of my life—and, believe me, that's saying something. You feel no compunction about that?'

'Did you hear what I said?' he demanded, after the smallest of pauses. 'You were a part of a plan to con me out of more than a billion dollars—that's tantamount to theft. As far as I'm concerned, you forfeited the right for any consideration.'

Her lips parted.

'I feel very sorry for you, Luca. To be so cynical at such a young age.' She shook her head. 'No one in my family intended to con you into anything. I don't know what you think you "discovered", but you're wrong. This was a business deal, pure and simple. We are a respectable family and you—you are nothing. *Niente!*' She slashed her hand through the air. 'No, you're worse. You are a bastard, and I can't stand the sight of you.' She pulled away and began to run, with no idea of where she was going, only absolutely certain that she needed to get away from him.

She had taken a path through the citrus grove, and towards the beach, but Luca hadn't followed immediately. He'd been frozen. With shock, but also with the emotions he'd thought he'd conquered as a young boy, when the children in his village called him *bastardo* as a running joke.

Bastardo. Bastard. The illegitimate son of a poor, struggling housekeeper, and no idea who for a father. The bullying had followed him all through primary school, until his mother had died and his father had come from the woodwork to claim him. But by then, the damage was done. Luca, rejected and ignored by his father, raised by a mother who couldn't look at him without seeing Carrick Stone and feeling the pain of his betrayal, and taunted by his contemporaries, Luca's heart had hardened a long time ago. And yet that single word, issued by Mia, cut him in a way he was truly surprised to feel.

He clenched his jaw and stared after Mia's retreating figure until she was no longer in sight.

She hadn't meant the word in the traditional sense. She'd intended it purely as an insult, as she might have chosen 'jackass' or any other not particularly flattering term to describe him and his behaviour.

And she wouldn't be one hundred per cent wrong.

Oh, he hadn't changed his opinion of her, nor her parents, but he wished he hadn't been drawn into that argument.

He didn't want to argue with Mia—there was

no point. Arguments were useful to clarify dis-agreements, in the spirit of seeking a more har-monious relationship, but Luca didn't intend to have a relationship with Mia beyond a few nights in bed together. It was very obvious to him that they both needed to work this out of their systems, and he presumed time here at the villa would be sufficient.

But once they returned to Palermo, that would be the end of it.

He might even leave the country again, to be sure.

A visit to Singapore was always nice—he had an office there and could lose himself in opera-tions for a while. Even Sydney, at a pinch. He'd avoid his father, see his brother. Perfect.

By the time his anger had simmered down and the wound from her insult had faded, Mia was long gone.

Discarding his jacket on the front steps of the house, he began to stride through the groves, in-stinctively heading to the beach. It was as good a place to check as any.

He found her there, but far away, her figure small as she walked too far, too fast, in the af-ternoon heat. He quickened his own step, eas-ily outstripping hers, until he was close enough to reach for her.

He grabbed her wrist, a hint of his anger returning, spun her around and then froze.

Because Mia Marini was *crying*. Actual tears. Her cheeks were wet with them.

It pulled at something in his gut, something he hadn't felt in a long time, something he really didn't like. He knew, with absolute certainty, how angry his mother would have been with him, for having made Mia cry. No matter what sins Mia had committed, Luca should have been better.

Don't stoop to their level, Luca amore.

Mia had been a part of a plan to effectively steal from him, but that didn't mean he needed to debase himself by hurtling insults at her feet.

'Just don't,' she groaned, pulling at her hand. He didn't let go. He couldn't. It was as if they were welded together.

'I don't want to fight with you,' he said, simply, frowning because it was absolutely true. 'That's not why I brought you here. The past is, as far as I am concerned, in the past.'

She shook her head. 'But we share a past, with very different opinions on it. That's important.'

'Not to me,' he said, pulling her to him. 'You made a mistake. I don't care any longer. I didn't marry you. I didn't buy the company. No harm was done. We have both moved on. Let's not discuss it again.'

She opened her mouth but he didn't want to hear it. It suddenly became very important to Luca that Mia not use those stunning lips to issue any more lies, and definitely no more defences of her parents. That was what bothered him most of all. That she'd been embroiled in the deception, and that she was attempting to excuse it now. Or worse, to still treat him like a fool, by refusing to admit the truth.

'But I haven't moved on,' she said, quietly. 'Not really, and you can't say that no harm was done, because it was. That day, when you didn't show up…'

He refused to react, but how could he not feel? Just a hint of compunction at that decision now, when faced with the obvious impact it had had on Mia?

Her eyes narrowed, tears still falling. 'When did you decide you wouldn't buy the company?'

His eyes roamed her face. 'It doesn't matter.'

'When?' She lifted a hand to his chest, imploring him to answer.

'I had just discovered the truth the last time I saw you. Earlier that day.'

'Truth,' she spat, then her eyes swept shut, shielding her thoughts and stories from him.

'You knew even then that you wouldn't marry me, didn't you?'

He didn't answer.

She blinked up at him, anguish in her features. 'You came to our house that night knowing you weren't going to go through with it?'

'I gave your father a chance to prove me wrong. He couldn't.'

She shook her head, frowning, so it was obvious to Luca that she didn't really accept the premise of that statement. 'And in the six days between that night and our wedding day, it didn't occur to you to tell me?'

He was very still. The world seemed strange.

At the time, he'd taken pleasure in simply walking away. They'd been a single team of people who'd conspired to trick him, to make a fool of Luca. Why give them the courtesy of civility? Luca had achieved what he'd achieved in life precisely by being ruthless in his approach to all things. Fair, ethical, but once wronged, he showed no mercy. That approach had served him well.

But now, standing opposite Mia, close to her, being forced to relive that day through her eyes, he had the very unpleasant experience of realising he'd taken it too far. It was one thing to defend your interests, another to wilfully harm another person.

And he had harmed Mia.

But didn't she deserve it? a voice in the back of his mind argued. Didn't her decision to get involved in the scam sale of the business negate any right to his compassion?

Evidently not, because he felt it now in abundance.

'I didn't think you would be hurt.'

More tears fell.

'I presumed your father must have told you about the business, that you would likely know what was coming.'

She shook her head. 'Did you see the photos of me?'

'Yes.' He'd been in the air at the time, flying from New York to San Francisco. His brother had emailed him.

'I was in a wedding dress. Waiting for you. And you just…you didn't arrive. You'd left the country the night before without so much as a goodbye text. I find it impossible to believe you just didn't think how your departure would affect me.' She sucked in a shaking breath. 'You *wanted* to hurt me. You wanted to inflict the most pain possible for whatever imagined wrong you felt had been done against you.' She blinked up at him, and those eyes stared into his, so layered with feeling that he took a step back, as though she'd pushed him again.

'I was very angry, Mia. You have to understand what my business means to me. I built this from scratch. I worked very hard to create my fortune and my success—it's more than money, it's more than that. Your parents wanted to take it all away from me—you did, too.'

'Tell me why you say that,' she pleaded. 'As far as I know, my father simply wants to sell the business because he is looking to retire. And he wants me to be a part of that, because I'm a Marini. At least, I am on paper,' she added with a shaking voice.

'You work in the business,' he said, needing to cling to what he had, for a year, considered to be the truth. Her working deep in the trenches of Marini Enterprises was further evidence of her involvement in the whole sordid scheme.

'So?' She lifted her shoulders. 'That's no guarantee that any new owner would keep me in the role—it's important to my father that a Marini remains in the company. Besides, it's about more than the business.' She frowned, trailing off, not answering his question.

She'd misunderstood him anyway, but he was glad, because he didn't want to put any more blame at her feet. He wasn't in the mood.

'I meant what I said, Mia.' He moved closer to her again, pulling her against his body, linking his hands in the small of her back. 'I didn't bring you here to argue over what happened then. As far as I'm concerned, that was then, this is now, and now, this, is what I'm interested in.'

She swallowed, her throat shifting. 'You mean sex?'

His eyes bored into hers. He didn't particularly like her description and yet, wasn't it the most accurate?

'Sure. Sex. Why not?'

'Because I'm engaged?'

He hadn't forgotten about Lorenzo, exactly, but Mia's fiancé was a thousand miles away from what Luca wanted to contemplate. When she lifted her hand to show him the sparkling diamond ring she wore, something strange filtered through him. He didn't want to see it. He knew she was planning to marry another man, someone else she didn't know, and didn't care for, but, for some reason, he didn't want it thrown in his face.

'And is marrying Lorenzo di Angelo really what you want with your life?'

She blinked up at him as though he'd sprouted three heads, and then she made a strange noise, dropping her head into her hands and laughing silently for a moment. Luca's heart squeezed tight.

'What I want doesn't matter. It's what has to happen,' she said, but through a sad, awful smile that pulled at his insides and made them hurt. She knew how bad their finances were, despite what she was trying to claim to him, that much was abundantly clear. Why else would she feel such a sense of obligation? This was the only way to save her parents from destitution.

'You are a free woman, Mia. You can do what you want.'

She lifted a brow. 'Says the man who kidnapped me?'

He ignored her accusation and the accompanying jab of guilt. 'Why must you marry him? This is the twenty-first century.'

'Yes, and I'm the overprotected only child of a very old, proud Sicilian family.' She shook her head. 'You couldn't possibly understand.'

A muscle jerked in his jaw as he tried not to let her throwaway rejoinder dig beneath his skin. 'Because of how I was raised?'

She furrowed her brow, shaking her head, looking confused, so he'd clearly read too much into her comment. 'No. Because you're not me. You don't know what it's like growing up as I did.' She bit down on her lip. 'My duty—and obligation—is to make them happy. It's the least I can do. Marrying Lorenzo will do that.' Her eyes were swirling with angst. He analysed her words, her statement—she would do anything her parents asked of her. Lie for them? Con him? 'It will fix everything that broke on our wedding day. I have to do this.'

The world tilted sideways, and his brain power, all of it, homed in on her final statement. He'd had no idea the ramifications of his rejection would be so intense for Mia. He'd thought her very much a part of the scheme to dupe him, but what if she hadn't been? What if she'd been innocently, blithely going along with her parents' plans and when those plans had fallen through, she'd been blamed?

'They cannot have thought it was your fault.'

Her eyes swept shut. She was pushing him away. His hands were clasped behind her back, he pulled them now, jerking her against him, demanding with his body that she face him, and this, head-on.

'They never said as much,' she admitted. 'But I felt it. I know how devastated they were, how completely blindsided we all were. Whatever you may think, my dad clearly had no idea you wouldn't go through with the wedding.'

'Then he's a fool.'

She blinked at him with consternation. Belatedly, he remembered what he'd said, about not discussing the past. He tried to pull the censure back from his tone, to focus on the present, and the future, but, in the back of his mind, how could he not dissect what she'd said? Mia had been a part of the deal he'd resented at first, but he'd wanted the company enough to go along with it. But then, as they'd spent time together, he'd been struck by how much he wanted her, by how drugging her company was. Which had made him even angrier when he'd learned the truth. If they'd shared no chemistry, if he hadn't been prepared to ignore his usual caution with relationships and jump into bed—and marriage—with her, maybe he would have cared less? But Mia had wronged him and he'd hated that. It had all seemed so right at the time but now he wasn't so sure, and Luca hated being uncertain about anything, least of all his decisions.

'So you're marrying Lorenzo to redeem yourself, in their eyes?'

'People get married for all sorts of reasons,' she said with quiet pride.

'Love is generally the most common.'

'This *is* about love,' she murmured, and he was very still, because that changed everything. Was he wrong about their relationship? Had she fallen in love with the other man? Were they actually a couple? Infidelity was not something Luca had any interest in, being, as he was, the by-product of a messy affair. 'Love for my parents,' she continued unevenly, eyes not meeting his. 'They're far from perfect, I know that, but they chose to adopt me, to raise me as their own, to give me every advantage they could in life. They're not perfect, but I care about them, I'm grateful to them, and I want—'

She broke off, eyes troubled when they lifted to his. She was nervous, not sure how to finish what she wanted to say, but he needed to hear it, because it seemed important, and he wanted to hear all her secrets, even when he could guess the conclusion to that. She loved her parents enough to do anything for them. Even commit criminal fraud. It hardened his voice, just a little. 'Yes?'

'I want them to be proud of me,' she finished softly, closing her eyes again, and then his heart seemed to split in two. He went from sitting in judgement of her to pitying her and hating her parents more than he already did. That they weren't already proud of her made him despise her parents more than previously, which was saying something.

'But it's more than that.' Her voice continued, and there was renewed strength in it, determination. 'I want freedom from them, too. My parents show love by exerting control. I'm twenty-three and they treat me like I'm a teenager. When I'm married, I'll move out. I'll have my own home, my own life, my own family.' She shrugged. 'Those seem like pretty good reasons to get married—even to someone I barely know. Don't you think?'

CHAPTER FIVE

MIA KNEW THAT, no matter what she might say to Luca, she was willing to go along with this the minute she sent the text message to her mother.

Have gone to Rome to meet with a potential buyer, I'll be back tomorrow.

It was a little white lie, a courtesy to Jennifer because if Mia simply didn't arrive home, Jennifer and Gianni would worry—and it was only a slight bending of the truth anyway, as Mia had indeed held an online meeting with a buyer in Rome that morning.

She tilted her face to the sun, the warmth almost unbearable. She had no spare clothes, and the outfit she'd worn to work that morning didn't exactly scream 'relaxing by the pool', but maybe that was a good thing? She didn't want Luca to know how readily she'd acceded to his heavy-handed plans. Perhaps her corporate clothes could be seen as a form of silent protest? Only, it really was very hot, and so, with a sigh, she finally gave in and removed her jacket, placing it over the back of one of the loungers. But that was as far as she intended to go in a concession to comfort!

'It's a private pool. A private beach.' He gestured behind them, and her eyes followed his hand, her heart tripping at the beauty of it all. 'You do not need bathers, *cara*.'

Her stomach swirled. This man had seen her naked. He'd worshipped her curves—not once had she felt as though he wished she were skinnier. But when she looked at him, in just a pair of black boxer briefs, so toned and tanned, she became self-conscious again, her mother's repeated barbs hitting their mark, even now, years later.

'I'm fine,' she said, prim-sounding. 'You go ahead.' She crossed her arms over her chest, seeking refuge in irritation rather than allowing herself to relax into this paradise.

'Suit yourself.' He shrugged before diving into the water, his dark head sleek when he emerged at the other end a moment later, his powerful body mesmerising as it tore through the water. He was built like a swimmer, she realised, with those broad shoulders and a slim, tapered waist, powerful legs, all lean and muscular. He looked completely at home in the water, like Poseidon, Greek God of the Sea. And Earthquakes, if she was remembering her ancient myths correctly. Which made a lot of sense, given how unstable the ground felt whenever she was near him.

Prevaricating a moment, she kicked off her shoes and placed them neatly beneath the lounger, then walked to the edge of the pool, choosing a part that wasn't splashed with water and sitting down, dangling her feet and calves in. It was divine. The perfect balm to such a warm day.

You've been kidnapped, her brain tried to remind her.

But there was a small part of Mia that wondered if maybe she hadn't actually been saved. For a moment, she rested back on her palms, face tilted to the sky, and pictured herself as some kind of modern-day Rapunzel, brought down from the tower and carried away on a horse. But Luca was no knight in shining armour, and she wasn't a damsel in distress. She was determined not to be. Mia was taking control of her own life and destiny. Marrying Lorenzo would be her ticket to freedom. She was going to make sure of it.

His hands around her calves jolted Mia out of her thoughts. She looked down at Luca and her heart skipped a beat. For one perfect moment, she let herself imagine that this was real.

That her other life had been a dream. An awful nightmare.

She imagined that Luca hadn't left her on their wedding day. That they'd married and lived here, just the two of them, in this picturesque paradise, far from her parents, from anything and anyone. She imagined that instead of marrying Lorenzo, she was already married to Luca. It was an illusion, a balloon she had to burst, and so she spoke quickly, needing to drag herself—even if inwardly kicking and screaming—back to reality.

'Where did you go anyway?'

His sexy smile made her blood pound. 'When?'

'The night before our wedding.'

His smile dropped. His face was thunder. He didn't want to answer.

'It's a straightforward question.'

His jaw was clenched. Perhaps he disagreed, but after a beat, he spoke. 'It's no secret. I went to America.'

'Why?'

'I have an office in New York.'

She furrowed her brow. 'And you suddenly needed to be there?'

'Is that so hard to believe?'

She tilted her lips to the side. 'Well, so far as I knew, you were planning to marry me.' A thought occurred to her, one that made ice trickle down her spine. 'You were going to marry me at some point, weren't you? You didn't set out from the beginning to humiliate me like that?'

'No, Mia, no. Up until I uncovered your father's…disingenuity, I believed you and I would marry. It was part of the deal.'

She nodded slowly. It should have mollified her, but hearing him describe their marriage as part of the deal—even when that was a very accurate assessment—made her insides hurt. 'But you didn't *want* to marry me.'

His eyes didn't quite meet hers. 'Before your father suggested it, I never intended to marry anyone.'

'So why agree to that term?'

'At the time, I wanted your father's business.'

'Enough to marry me?'

He moved between her legs, and now, when their eyes locked, sparks flooded her blood. 'I wanted his business more than almost anything in the world.'

Her eyes swept shut. 'I see. So what changed?'

He didn't answer the question. 'About ten years earlier, my father had tried to purchase it,' he admitted, voice rough. 'He failed. Your father wouldn't sell. My father was...displeased. He takes all corporate losses seriously. I enjoyed the prospect of succeeding where he'd failed.' He confessed the truth without a hint of apology.

Mia considered that carefully. 'You don't get on with your father?'

Luca's lips twisted into that now-familiar mocking smile. 'No.'

She shivered involuntarily but before she could probe further, Luca changed the subject. 'Prior to your father proposing the term, I had no intention of marrying, Mia. I have never wanted a wife.'

'So why did you agree to it?'

He eyed her carefully, probing, and then shrugged his broad shoulders. 'Because I met you,' he answered after a beat. Her heart stammered. Was this the truth?

'And I was intrigued.'

He lifted a hand, trailed water over her thigh. She shivered. 'Do you remember that evening?'

She bit into her lip. 'Dinner with my parents? Of course I do.' She remembered everything about it, from Luca's late arrival, his arrogant features, but then...he'd looked at her and time had seemed to stand still. When he'd held out his hand to shake hers, Mia had felt as though everything was falling into place. She was no longer afraid of the proposed wedding. She was no longer anxious about the future. There was something about him she'd instantly trusted and liked. And the desire that had overheated her insides hadn't hurt.

Had he felt it too?

'You were so beautiful, and so enigmatic. Your mother spoke all evening. Even when I asked you a question, she answered, so I found myself quite desperate to get you alone.'

Mia made a sound of surprise.

'But I couldn't; not then. I felt as though they were keeping me away from you on purpose, to make me mad with desire, so that I would agree to almost anything to marry you.'

'As if,' she said with a roll of her eyes. 'No one in my family has that inflated view of my abilities to appeal.'

His brow lifted cynically. 'I have spent the last year believing you played your part to perfection, but now...'

'Now?' she asked, breathlessly, leaning forward unconsciously.

'I think I was wrong. About you,' he clarified quickly, letting his fingers drop to her skin above her knee, then lower, to her calf.

Pleasure swirled inside her, but Mia tried not to let it alter her resolve. Whatever he'd felt, he'd had no right to simply disappear from their wedding day.

'What did you imagine our marriage would have been like, Mia?'

She hesitated a moment. 'I—I'm not sure.' She didn't want to admit to the fantasies she'd allowed to run rampant through her mind. 'I didn't really think about that.'

'You agreed to marry me,' he pointed out quietly. 'So what would you have *wanted* that marriage to look like?'

'I've told you what I wanted,' she murmured. 'To make my parents proud. To escape. To gain a degree of independence.'

'And from your husband? Simply a roof over your head?'

She still wouldn't look at him, and Luca, using those powerful arms, pulled out of the water to sit beside her, dripping wet. He'd placed himself directly in her line of sight, his face only an inch from hers. The water droplets beaded across his face. She ached to reach out and lick them.

It made her mouth dry and her cheeks heat.

'Mia?' He caught her chin, lifting her face, holding her gaze locked to his.

'What I want—what I've always wanted—is a family of my own. I never expected...for a long time, my parents have spoken about finding me a suitable husband, someone of whom they approved, who my biological parents would have approved of too.' Her brow crinkled, and, in the back of her mind, she wondered when she'd become okay with that. 'It wasn't like I had dreams of growing up and falling in love. But I always knew I wanted children of my own. Lots of children.' Her lips were twisted in a strange smile. 'I would have settled for two, though. A boy and a girl, if I could prescribe such things.'

He was very still, watchful, his eyes probing hers, and when he spoke, his voice had a strange, heavy resonance. 'Then it's just as well we didn't marry, Mia, because I have always known, since I was a boy, that I would not have children.'

Her heart stammered and her stomach rolled like the motion of a dolphin dipping beneath the ocean. 'You can't?'

'No. Not can't. I won't.'

'Why not?' It made no sense to Mia. She couldn't fathom his feelings; not even a little.

'Why do you want children?'

She toyed with her fingers. *Because I'm an only child. Because I was adopted. Because I desperately wanted siblings. Because I want actual unconditional love.* There were any number of reasons she could have chosen, but instead, she lifted her shoulders. 'I just know I want them.'

'Just as I know I don't.'

He was right, then, she realised with a leaden feeling. It was for the best that they hadn't married. But it felt like the slamming shut of a door she realised she still wanted open. Ridiculous. Their 'marriage' hadn't happened. He'd humiliated her, made her a laughing stock. And now she was marrying someone else. Someone kind and gentle who didn't intimidate her at all, who she suspected she could twist around her little finger. Most importantly, she was marrying someone who came from a big family and had willingly agreed to Mia's stipulation that they would have children. Not straight away, but within a couple of years, when she was ready.

Why hadn't she thought to make such a stipulation with Luca?

Had she been so swept up in the idea of becoming his wife that she'd been happy to leave such things to chance? Or had she just presumed that he'd feel as she did? Had she taken it for granted that everyone must have such strong feelings on family?

'Then I guess it all worked out for the best,' she said, wondering if her voice sounded as brittle to him as it did to her. 'I could never have been happily married to you.'

Silence fell. A strange, weighted silence.

'And Lorenzo?' he prompted.

She forced a smile, hoped it seemed genuine. 'He wants children, too.'

'You've discussed it?'

'Yes.'

A frown flickered on Luca's brow, like lightning, quick but obvious. 'How well do you know him?'

She shrugged again. 'We've met a few times. I learned from our engagement.' She gestured towards Luca. 'I wanted to know—'

Luca stared at her, silent. Somehow that silence was deafening.

She sighed. 'I wanted to be sure he wouldn't...'

She didn't finish the sentence, but she didn't need to. He seemed to understand anyway. Luca tilted her chin once more, bringing their faces together. 'I had no intention of hurting you.'

Her lips pulled to the side. 'I think you did,' she said softly, slowly. 'I think you believed I deserved it, though.'

His eyes narrowed and Mia's heart twisted. She was so confused. When she was with Luca, she wanted to slam shut the door on the rest of the world and exist purely in this space, purely with him. But she couldn't forget how he'd treated her, and her parents, how he'd hurt her. She'd gone to him last night with the intention of hurting him back. Of giving him a taste of his own medicine. And instead, she'd fallen more under his spell than ever. What else could explain her willingness to sit beside him and calmly discuss their almost-wedding day?

'Yes.' His response was quiet. 'I did.'

Her eyes lifted to his, sadness in their depths. 'And now?'

He captured her face with his hands, holding her cheeks, moving closer, brushing her lips with his. 'The past is immaterial,' he said, except it wasn't.

'Not to me.' She pulled back, just a fraction, so she could say what was on her mind. 'That day changed me, Luca. You changed me. When you walked out on our wedding and left me like that, it fundamentally altered who I am. Probably for the better,' she added after a beat. 'I'm less trusting, less gullible, more careful to look after myself. That's *not* immaterial.'

'Mia.' He said her name on a groan, then pulled her back to him, kissing her hard, fast, hungrily, perhaps to silence her? To stop her enumeration of all the ways his behaviour had affected her?

It suddenly became imperative to Mia to make him understand how she felt—what she knew to be the truth. 'You're not safe, Luca,' she said quickly, against his lips. 'You're not good for me. When we go back to Palermo, I can't see you again. I'm getting married. This has to be the end of us.'

His response was to bring his wet, beautiful body over hers and kiss her senseless, until white-hot need drove them inside, to his bedroom, and the essential supply of contraceptives he kept there. But Mia, by then, was too saturated in pleasure to care.

'You're not safe, Luca. You're not good for me.'
Her words played over and over in his mind like an awful song he couldn't switch off. Back at home in Palermo, he heard her voice, the sad yet determined tone, and wanted to reach out and kiss her again, to kiss away that pain and, indeed, the entire sentiment.

Luca had no fantasy of being any woman's saviour. He'd assiduously avoided relationships, rarely got involved with the opposite sex. He dated, from time to time, but he was always careful to manage expectations. His mother had driven that lesson into him. Not by anything she'd said directly, but whenever she'd refer to his father, it was always with that wistful, love-lorn look in her eyes, so Luca had grown up understanding the truth: she'd loved Luca's father, he hadn't loved her back. He hadn't wanted any part of their family, because he'd already had a family of his own. A family who could never know the truth. And so Luca's mother had moved them down to Sicily, where she had family, in an attempt to hide Luca away, and Luca had grown up understanding more than any little boy should ever have to.

While he had no fantasy of becoming Mia's knight in shining armour, nor did he want to be her villain.

Somewhere along the way, he'd promised himself he would never be like his father, leaving a string of broken hearts in his wake. He'd promised himself he would act according to his strict moral code, a black and white system of right and wrong, and he had. Even his departure from Italy had, at the time, met that criteria: *an eye for an eye.*

He had no doubt Mia's parents had been scamming him. The business figures were fraudulent. They'd lied to make Marini Enterprises appear far more profitable than it was, and perhaps they'd been hoping he'd be so fascinated by the silent, enigmatic, beautiful Mia that he wouldn't notice—or care. He'd naturally presumed she'd been a part of the deception.

And if she hadn't?

Not *if.* He knew she hadn't.

Mia just wasn't capable of that kind of deceit. She was all that was decent and good. Which meant her parents had used her, too. Perhaps out of love, out of a desire to see her taken care of, as she'd said. Or maybe it was more sinister?

Either way, on the eve of his wedding, he'd taken great satisfaction in leaving the country without an explanation. But now, a year later, her words were a form of torture because they forced him to reckon with the fact he'd made a mistake. He'd acted out of his unfailing black and white morality but he'd been wrong. Whatever trouble her parents' business was in, whatever means they were using in order to sell it without disclosing the true financial situation, Mia wasn't complicit in that and never had been. She'd agreed to marry first him and now Lorenzo out of a sense of love for her parents, and a duty to them that was completely unreasonable, and he'd only made everything worse for her.

But could he see her again—as he desperately wanted to—without hurting her? Could he do this and protect her? Luca knew he had nothing to offer Mia long term. He wasn't interested in a real relationship, and marriage wasn't on his radar. Children were unequivocally off the table. So in going to Mia, he had to make sure he didn't do anything that would jeopardise her plans, that would make life more difficult for her than it already was. What she did with herself next wasn't Luca's concern—

he wanted her in the here and now, but Mia's future was her own to plan for.

'You can't be here.' It was one of those instances where her words were at complete odds with her feelings. She was scandalised and terrified, but also exhilarated. Luca appearing in her office was both incredibly stupid and…everything she'd been wanting, since coming back from San Vito Lo Capo two days earlier, feeling as though she were missing a limb.

'You left me no choice,' he responded with a sardonic drawl.

Heat bloomed in Mia's cheeks as she moved quickly to the door of her office and closed it, swooshing down the venetian blinds. Everything felt smaller with him in this space. He stood with feet planted wide apart, so he was like a statue made of stone in the centre of the room, and she was torn between wanting to run towards him to embrace him, or to push him over.

Her fingers shook as adrenaline rushed through her body.

'This is my office. My father works two doors down. He could have *seen* you.'

'I waited until he left,' Luca said, arms crossed over his chest.

She gaped. 'Luca—'

His nostrils flared. 'What we do with our time is our business.'

'How do you do that?'

'Do what?'

'Make it all sound so easy,' she said, pressing her fingertips to her forehead and then, as if it were a talisman, holding her hand towards him, displaying the large engagement ring she wore. 'I'm getting married.'

Luca's expression didn't alter, his appearance didn't change. 'To a man you barely know and don't care about.'

She let out a deranged half-laugh. 'Yes. That's true. But I am *getting married* and you know why. And you're—'

He moved closer, putting his hands on her cheeks, just like at the beach, so she felt safe and valued and calm even as a storm raged in her chest. 'What am I?'

'I am so angry at you,' she said honestly, because she needed to cling to that. 'For what you did a year ago. I can't forgive it.'

His eyes held hers but they were impossible to read, despite the strength of their connection. 'I'm not asking for your forgiveness.'

Of course he wasn't. Luca wasn't a man who cared for the good opinion of others. What did it matter to Luca Cavallaro how Mia felt about him? His sense of self was far too assured for her feelings to have any impact.

'Then what are you asking for? What do you want from me?' She lifted a hand to his chest. 'What do you want from me?' she repeated, groaning, because she'd been going crazy with wanting him and suddenly, she didn't care about anything except the fact he was here and seemed to need her as she needed him.

'One week.' He pushed her backwards, pressing his body to her, so she was caught between the edge of her desk and his strong thighs, and her world began to crumble and tumble and roll, her eyes filled with stars and fireworks and flame. 'Give me one week of your time, Mia. Let me have you, just for one week.'

'And then what? You've had me already for two days. Was that not enough?' She needed to know.

'I'll go away again. I'll stay away.'

She swallowed, trembling, tortured and delighted in equal measure. He was offering something so simple. A week. A week out of time, to enjoy him and this and then return to normal. With a set-in-stone end point to their fling, surely that would limit any potential harm.

He moved his mouth to the corner of hers, kissing her there lightly, making it hard to think clearly.

'Nobody can ever know.' She tried to cling to sense, to hold onto rational thought for long enough to negotiate this in a meaningful way, to make the kinds of stipulations she should have made in the first instance, way back when they were engaged. But in the last year, Mia had grown, and she'd changed, and that meant being more determined to stand up for herself and what she wanted.

'I am not intending to take out an advertisement.'

'I mean it, Luca.' She pulled back to stare into his eyes. 'You pulled my life apart once— you can't do it again. You have to play by the rules. *My* rules.'

His eyes narrowed slightly. 'And what are they?'

Given the opportunity to enumerate a list, she found her mind becoming blank. But she waded through the flotsam and forced herself to focus. 'We have to keep this secret. No being seen together in public, no turning up at my office,' she added quickly. 'No following me to bridal-dress fittings. No going out for dinners, nothing like that. My parents know everybody in Sicilia, just about, and those they don't, Lorenzo's family will know. Nowhere is safe.'

'Except my home,' he pointed out.

A thrill of excitement exploded inside Mia's chest. 'Yes,' she conceded carefully.

'Any other rules?'

'One week,' she said emphatically, because she needed to cement that in her own mind. 'Nothing beyond it. This is an aberration. I want to focus on my new life and I can't do that when you're here. So after a week, you'll go, just like you said.'

He nodded curtly. 'I've already agreed to this.'

'You also agreed to marry me,' she reminded him, then winced, because she was sick of dragging up the past, of remembering that hurt. 'But we both know it's a good thing you didn't.'

Silence sparked in the air. 'Now, it's my turn.'

'For what?'

'Rules. I will do everything I can to ensure no one learns about this,' he promised. 'But you are completely and utterly mine for the next week. Do or say whatever you need, but you will be in my bed, at my home, for the next seven days.'

Her eyes widened and her mouth parted. Terror and delight were tangling in her belly. It sounded so wonderful, so heavenly, but it wasn't reality. 'I can't...'

He pressed a finger to her lips. 'We have one week. You *can*.'

She thought of some options, desperation

making her like a descendent of Machiavelli suddenly. 'I'll try,' she said with a nod, thinking of her best friend, the one friend of Mia's who her parents actually approved of. Mia had mentioned a desire to travel to London to spend some time with Caroline—she could fib and say she was going, spur of the moment, next week. Excitement pounded in her chest.

'Anything else?' She was breathless.

He lifted up, eyes sparking with hers. 'No.' He ground his hips against her and she whimpered, because he was hard and she was desperately hungry for him after two days of not seeing him. 'My car will collect you on the corner. Don't keep me waiting too long, Mia.'

'I won't.'

'Promise?'

Everything slowed down until the world stopped spinning. Standing on a precipice, Mia knew she should hesitate, that doubts should be flooding her, but the truth was, everything suddenly seemed so simple and *right*. 'I promise,' she agreed huskily, and she really, really did.

CHAPTER SIX

MIA HAD EXPECTED the car to take them to Luca's Palermo town house but instead, within ten minutes of leaving the office, they were on their way down a familiar road, out of the city, towards San Vito Lo Capo, and Mia was glad. Glad because Palermo felt risky even within the confines of his home, and because what they were doing was such a slice out of time that it felt better to be also out of space, out of her familiar geographical locations.

'I have no clothes except these,' she said with a tilt of her lips.

'You will not need clothes,' he drawled, reaching across and wrapping his hand over her thigh.

Anticipation flooded Mia's veins. 'Luca...' Her breath hitched. What had she wanted to say?

'I have arranged everything. Trust me.'

Her eyes flicked to his and then away again, a frown tugging at her lips.

He was the stuff of fantasies, but surely not a man to be trusted after what happened a year ago, and Mia needed to remember that. She had to keep her wits about her, to limit what they were doing to the incredible, mind-blowing sex, and nothing more. This wasn't her real life.

They arrived at the villa as the sun was dipping low in the sky and it was the most stunningly picturesque view, the gradients quite mesmerising. She stood on the front step, staring outwards, towards the mountains that were welcoming the sun with open arms for a night's rest, and sighed.

The future was murky, but, right now, everything was just as it needed to be. Recognising that unlocked a part of her to fully enjoy this. She couldn't marry Lorenzo without getting Luca fully out of her system. It wouldn't have been fair to Lorenzo or herself to bring this kind of desire for another man into their marriage. So she'd enjoy this week with Luca and happily farewell him at the end of it, ready to move on with her life and put Luca where he belonged: properly in the past. But rather than thinking of him and feeling a sense of rejection and hurt, she'd look back at what they'd shared as the birth of something within Mia—

her sensual awakening, her self-confidence as a woman. These were aspects of Mia that had been totally neglected.

She would always be grateful to Luca for drawing them into the light.

'Ready?' He reached down and linked their fingers. She stared at the sky a moment longer, thinking about sunsets and endings and the promise of new beginnings, and then turned, blinked up at him as if seeing Luca for the first time, because if she was completely his for the next week then he was also completely hers.

'Yes,' came the breathy response.

'Good. Because I know just what I want to do with you first.'

Her heart was pounding as he led her through the beautiful old villa, but rather than guiding Mia to the bedroom they'd shared a few nights ago, he showed her out onto the terrace, to the stunning infinity pool with views towards the orange-hued sky, and darkening ocean.

'Turn around.' His voice was thick, hoarse.

She did as he said, her heart pounding. His fingers caught the zip at the top of her back and drew it down, loosening the dress she wore, until it fell away from her body altogether, leaving her exposed in just her underwear. She was outside, visible to the world, and yet the world couldn't see into the villa—it was, as Luca had told her, a completely private stretch of beach, there was no need to feel embarrassed, and yet usually Mia would have been riddled with self-consciousness. Only something about Luca, and the way he responded to her, was empowering and intoxicating and for the first time in her adult life she revelled in her nakedness, in being naked for him.

There was a rustle of clothing and then Luca's naked body was at her back, holding her, arms around her waist a moment, chin pressed to her shoulder. She trembled, knees weak. He removed her bra and underpants and Mia felt a thrill of power.

'You are beautiful,' he said with wonder, turning her to face him, eyes hooded. 'So beautiful. And all mine.'

'For one week,' she reminded him firmly, warmth spreading through her. When he called her beautiful, she really believed it. Years of conditioning by her mother seemed to ebb away.

His eyes flared and then he lifted her, holding her against his chest, carrying her towards the pool and stepping in. He was so strong. Not once did he appear to struggle, to stumble, but rather stepped easily, down, and down again, until Mia was enveloped by the delightfully warm water and sensations flooded her from head to toe—

his nakedness, so close, his warmth, the water, it was all utterly mind-blowing.

And when he kissed her, she was already at a fever pitch, the whirlpool of longing having begun to swirl from the moment he walked into her office, and it hadn't stopped all afternoon. When he kissed her, she felt beautiful, she felt warm all over, she felt like the most precious, fragile yet strong person in the world, and she never wanted it to stop—not now, and deep down, Mia admitted only to her most secret self, not even in a week.

Their hands were laced on the top of the table as the older woman brought out a platter of risotto, scampi and salad.

'My housekeeper,' Luca had said on Mia's last visit, when the sound of the door closing had alerted them to someone else being in their space and Mia had panicked. 'When I am at the villa, she comes for two hours each night. She can be trusted, Mia. She's worked for me a long time, and before that she was a friend of my mother's. She will not tell a soul that you are here.'

There was that word again: *trust*.

Mia smiled at the older woman as she bustled about with a wine bottle and then, when they were alone once more on the starlit terrace, the smell of night-flowering jasmine and honeysuckle heavy in the air, Mia pulled her hand back, flexing her fingers a little to remove the tingling effect of Luca's touch, and fixed him with a level stare.

'Do *you* trust her?'

His eyes locked to Mia's, then he reached for his wine glass, taking a sip of the crisp, white liquid before responding. 'Catarina? With my life.'

Mia frowned.

'You weren't expecting that answer?'

'No.' She speared a scampi and tasted it. Delicious.

'Because…' he prompted, when Mia didn't respond.

Her lips tugged to one side. 'You don't strike me as a man who trusts anyone.' She thought about that a little more. 'Or who lets people get close.'

'You're close. Look.' He reached out and touched her under the table.

Mia smiled but rolled her eyes. 'You know that's not what I mean.'

He sipped his wine, said nothing more.

'So?' she asked, leaning forward, elbows on the table, no longer interested in the food, though it was absolutely spectacular.

'What do you want to know?' There was a

guardedness to his voice, a wariness about what she might ask him, and how he might answer.

Mia didn't back down.

She had a limited time to get this man out of her system and that meant coming to understand him, because she didn't want to find herself thinking about him in six months' time, wondering what made him tick, what made him a certain way.

'Why?'

'Why?' He let out a sound of exasperated amusement. 'That's unquantifiable. A thousand things happen in a person's life that cause them to behave or feel a certain way, it's rarely just one.'

'And I'm asking about yours.'

'Why?'

'Well, because I'm here for a week and we can't be in bed the entire time,' she pointed out, cheeks blushing.

'Is that a challenge?'

She dipped her gaze to the table. 'I want to understand you, Luca.'

He reached over and lifted her chin. Mia's eyes hooked to his and her heart lurched in her chest. 'That wasn't part of the deal.'

Did he really mean to keep her at arm's length emotionally while physically exploiting all of their chemistry?

'Is this what you do with women?' She changed tack. 'Have sex but refuse to talk?'

'I'm happy to talk.'

'About things that matter.'

His eyes were hooded, no longer easy for Mia to comprehend, but they were darkened by emotion, so she wished she had the key to understanding. She wished she knew him better.

'I don't have serious relationships.' He removed his hand, returned it to his wine glass, sipped, swallowed, his Adam's apple drawing her attention to his throat. 'It wouldn't be fair.'

'No?' She was glad that he'd at least expanded a little on his answer.

'Why date when you have no intention of marriage?'

'You aren't unique in that respect, Luca. I'm sure there are lots of women who would be happy to spend time with you without wanting more.' Even as she said it, she suspected that was false. Of course that wasn't the case. Even women who might have felt they were anti-marriage or long-term commitment couldn't fail to be tempted by Luca. *And you?* a voice inside Mia jeered. After all, what insurance policy did Mia have against wanting more from him? More than this week?

Her eyes dropped to her engagement ring and she stared at it with a rush of relief. That was her insurance policy, her real life. Her duty. Her obligation. Even if she decided she wanted more from Luca, she couldn't have it, because she *needed* to marry Lorenzo. She'd promised her parents, and they had stressed to her how important the wedding was, as well as the sale of the business. Her father was desperate to retire, desperate enough to sell the family business, but only if Mia was a part of the deal, so that she would retain an interest in the ongoing success of the company her great-grandparents had built from nothing. She reminded herself it wasn't a love match. And Lorenzo knew that too. It was a mutually beneficial marriage on paper.

Something fuzzed at the edges of her mind, something dark and ominous that tightened her stomach into knots, but she couldn't quite grab hold of it. Her father had been stressed lately. Was it any wonder? After the debacle of the last would-be sale and wedding, he probably had the same form of stress echoes that Mia did.

'I have a policy of not stringing women along. I see women, when it suits me, but I don't date often, and I am always careful not to make any promises of more than I intend to offer.' He replaced the wine glass carefully. 'Personal conversation isn't...necessary.'

She frowned. 'So you'll sleep with them but not talk?'

'It works for me.'

She angled her face towards the dark sky over the shimmering, black ocean. 'I don't know why, but that makes me feel kind of sad for you.'

He didn't respond immediately. 'There's no need. My life is just how I like it.'

She nodded, because of course that was true. Just because Mia would find his type of intimacy hollowing, didn't mean he felt the same way.

They were different creatures, and it barely seemed to matter, because after this week, they'd cease to know one another at all.

Mia slept late the next day, which was hardly a surprise, given that she hadn't actually fallen asleep until well into the early hours of the morning.

Their agreement had unleashed something within them—a new sense of urgency, because they'd defined what they were and delineated how long they'd be this for. Both knew an end point was looming and seemed determined not to waste a moment.

It was exhaustion that had finally drawn Mia into sleep, when her eyes had grown too heavy and her body, her over-sensitised body, had felt unnaturally heavy, and Luca had gently pulled her to his chest, one big, strong arm clamped around her shoulders, and held her there, so the last thing she was aware of as she fell asleep was the beating of his heart.

He swam from one side of the cove to the other, as he did most mornings while at the villa, the workout and seawater a perfect way to energise his body for the day ahead. Usually, he then had a light breakfast and went to work in his study, so he could have been anywhere in the world—his Milan office, New York, Singapore, Sydney. They all had the same décor, the same equipment, to avoid the jarring sense of being out of routine.

But he didn't feel like working today.

He wanted Mia.

He swam harder, anger fuelling his strokes because he'd spent hours pleasuring her and surrendering to the pleasure she gave last night and it was almost unnatural that his body should still yearn for her with this blinding intensity, and yet it was all he could think of, all he wanted.

Mia was an anchor, drawing on him, even as he swam. In line with the house, he stopped, stood against the sandy bottom of the ocean with hands on his hips and stared at the building, trying to picture her, wondering what she was doing, imagining her naked body, those beautiful curves against the black silk of his sheets, her honey-coloured limbs tangled in the fabric, her hands wandering, exploring, touching herself because she'd awoken hungry for him, too.

Grinding his teeth, he began to stride from the ocean, intent on reaching the house by the shortest means available and, as quickly as possible thereafter, Mia. In the back of his mind, he had a virtual whiteboard and on it was written, in big red letters, six more nights.

He had no intention of wasting them.

The boat was everything she might have expected someone like Luca to possess—luxurious, fast, glistening white and chrome with very black windows and a sleek frame, and he drove the thing with expert ease, wearing just a pair of navy-blue shorts, so Mia found herself trying to focus on the beautiful coastline and, instead, unable to tear her eyes from his body.

Strange how these waters had once been a place of deep self-loathing and dread for Mia, and now, as Luca navigated through them, she felt an unbending need to ask him to stop the boat and let her off, to dive deep beneath the calm, crystalline surface, to be engulfed by this bay, its healing powers making her see herself as Luca claimed to. To feel truly beautiful. To erase all of the insults her mother had gently and cleverly woven into Mia's being, over all the years of her life.

They were far from land, far enough that she could see it as a postcard, all the tiny homes and the streets that lined the seafront, with their brightly coloured shops, restaurants with umbrellas, gelaterias bustling with queues of people in this midday heat. She sighed, reclined on her bed and reached for the lemon water Luca had brought her, a half-smile on her lips.

'You're lost in thought.'

Her eyes flicked to his. 'I suppose I am.'

'About?' There was a seriousness to his voice, as though he wasn't sure he'd like the answer.

She turned back to the water, the stunning turquoise ocean, and ran her fingers lightly over the arm of her daybed. 'I was reflecting on how different it is being back here with you, from when I used to come as a girl. I mean, obviously it's different.' Her cheeks blushed. 'But how I feel… I feel…happy.'

He frowned. 'You weren't happy then?'

Her lips pulled to the side. 'I thought you didn't do serious conversations.'

He hesitated a moment. 'Would you prefer not to talk about it?'

She laughed softly. 'I don't want to drag you into unfamiliar waters,' she said with a shake of her head. 'Forget it. It doesn't matter.'

Silence fell between them, and Mia presumed the conversation was closed, but then Luca reached out and squeezed her hand. 'I want to know. Tell me what you're thinking.'

It was nothing. Perhaps he was just being polite? But to Mia, something in her chest exploded and she couldn't say why.

She blinked away from him, staring at the crystal-clear waters.

'It would be a good idea for you to skip breakfasts for a while, Mia. Particularly those heavy English cooked ones.'

'We used to come here on summer vacations, to this exact place,' she said, softly, her words barely carrying to him in the afternoon sunshine. 'I loved it. As a girl, I would lose myself in the water for hours, emerging only when my skin was wrinkled like a prune and my eyes bleary from a combination of sunscreen and salt water.'

He squeezed her hand. 'And then, when I was about eleven, it started to change. I got heavier. Awkward. I'd come back from school and Mum would weigh me, frown, shake her head, tell me she was going to call the dorm mistress to speak about my diet.' Mia's voice was thick with emotion; she didn't look at Luca, didn't see the way his eyes sparked with a mix of anger and surprise.

'Swimming became a form of hell. She'd criticise my body as soon as I emerged from my room. I felt so self-conscious. I mean, your body's starting to change at that age and that's hard to get used to, but to have Mum draw my attention to it, as well as whoever else happened to be on the boat, it was excruciating. I stopped wanting to swim. I stopped wearing anything that showed skin. Eventually, I got out of coming on these trips altogether. But that didn't matter. Whether it was here or at home, Mum never let me forget what a disappointment I was because I wasn't like her.'

Luca stood, prowling to the edge of the boat, staring out at the sea, his back turned and ramrod straight, his shoulders taut. She found it easier to talk to his back, anyway.

'My mother is very beautiful and fashion is her favourite hobby. She would bemoan how unfortunate it was that none of her clothes would ever fit me, that they couldn't be passed down. She'd hoped to have a daughter she could share a wardrobe with, but instead she adopted me, and I was short and round.' Mia mimicked her mother's voice then closed her eyes, mortified to be revealing this much to Luca.

He spun around sharply, staring at Mia, his jaw clenched. 'Mia, you are beautiful. I say that not as a man who's become obsessed by your body, obsessed with making love to you, but as an objective stranger. When I first met you, I couldn't get you out of my head. You *know* that.'

She shook her head, struggling to accept that he'd felt as crazy with lust as she had. And yet, didn't she have more than enough evidence of that? Everything about his behaviour in the past week demonstrated that his own infatuation was at a fever-pitch level, like hers.

'It's hard to explain,' she said after a beat. 'It's not about whether her remarks had any basis in reality, but how they made me feel.'

'I can imagine,' he grunted. 'What kind of bitch goes out of her way to destroy a vulnerable teenager's self-esteem?'

She lifted her shoulders.

'I honestly think she meant well. She wanted to encourage me to lose weight—I'm not like her, so much as my biological mother, which makes a lot of sense, really.'

His eyes narrowed. 'Why the hell should weight loss be any kind of goal?'

She swallowed, and the academic part of her brain knew that he was right, that it was her mother who had been wrong to criticise and undermine Mia. 'Beauty is important to her.'

'Mia, listen to me. Let's set aside for a moment the indisputable fact that you are very beautiful and focus on something else. Would you like to know what I think happened?'

Mia nodded her head once, and Luca came to sit beside her, on the lounger, his body so close she felt his warmth wrapping around her. 'I believe you went away one year as a little girl and then came back showing the woman you'd become, and your mother was jealous. Because you're young and gorgeous and suddenly she realised she'd have competition. I have known women like her, who can't bear to be outshone, even by their own family members. That's her sickness, not yours. Don't take on her wounds and make them your own.'

She stared at him as if he were divining a lightning rod, right into her soul. Could this be true? Was her mother actually jealous of Mia?

'Not only are you beautiful, you shine from the inside out.' He pressed a hand to her chest. 'You shimmer with life. Happiness, joy, light and kindness, qualities that your mother could never experience as you do. Do not give her opinions any more room in your head, *cara*. You deserve better.'

When he said it, she found it so easy to believe. She felt as though a weight she'd been carrying for a million years were lifting off her, as if she could breathe properly for the first time in for ever.

'It's not like I care about looks,' she said, brow scrunching, because she wanted him to understand her. 'It's not a question of vanity. It's—a question of value. Self-worth.'

'You've lost weight,' he said slowly, as if the words were dredged from deep in his chest. 'Since our wedding.'

'There was no wedding.' She pulled her hand away, the memory of that day incongruous with the warmth and contentment he'd just poured through her. 'And it wasn't intentional.'

'I would hate to think you have been suffering under the misapprehension that what happened that day had anything to do with your appearance, and my lack of desire for you.'

She blanched, shaking her head. 'Can we really, please, seriously not talk about this?'

'Mia, it's important.'

'It really isn't,' she pleaded. 'In the scheme of things, what I think about this, how I feel, it just doesn't matter.'

'To me, it does.'

'Why?' she challenged with an urgency that came right from the very middle of her chest. 'Why do you even care, Luca?' She stood up, frustrated, pacing to the other side of the deck, staring out at the familiar view, hands clenched around the railing. 'You're the one who told me you don't do serious conversations. So why are you pushing this? Why can't you just let it go?' Her voice cracked. 'Please, would you just let it go?'

'I will.' He was speaking to her so softly, gently, as though she were a child. She compressed her lips, frustration making her nerve-endings reverberate. 'When you've explained this to me, I will never speak of it again.'

Her eyes glimmered with mutinous annoyance. 'That hardly sounds like a victory for me.'

'Why won't you discuss it?'

'Because it's in the past and because it hurts. Why dredge up something painful?'

'If it is pain that I caused, then I have a right to know about it.'

'God, Luca! What do you want me to say? That you not showing up for our wedding didn't impact me at all? That there were no negative consequences from that day?' She shook her head to dispel both sentiments. 'It was a disaster. You humiliated me. Worse, you confirmed every negative feeling I had about myself, every sentiment my mother had ever expressed to me. I felt worthless and unwanted and laughable. A total joke. Is it any wonder I'm a different person now? And I don't mean physically, I mean all of me.'

She tilted her chin with outraged defiance, hoping he could see the strength and determination that fired from her eyes. 'I fully believe you had no intention of hurting me, that you didn't even think about me as an individual, so much as a part of a business deal you no longer wanted any part of, but your actions that day broke me. I swore I'd never admit that to you,' she muttered. 'I swore I'd never let you know...'

'Don't.' He moved across the boat, drawing her into his arms. 'Don't lie to me any more, don't hide from me. I deserve to know what happened.' He drew in a deep breath, eyes swirling with feeling as they stared at each other. 'You're right,' he admitted gruffly, after a beat. 'I didn't think of you as an individual. Not really. But I didn't walk away because I didn't desire you, Mia. It had nothing to do with that. If anything, how I felt about you, how attracted I was to you, scared the hell out of me. It still does.'

He pressed a finger to her chin and she trembled, his words making no sense and all the sense in the world because this was *terrifying*. 'I walked out on our wedding because of your parents' actions. Not yours.'

She closed her eyes, hating their past, hating how much she wanted him, how complicated everything was.

'I worked hard to build my fortune, my life, to get out of the slums of Sicily, to prove to my father that I was more than he'd ever thought, more than the boy he spent twelve years ignoring. It's never been about money. It's so much more than that. The idea of someone trying to cheat me out of what I've achieved—I was enraged. You bore the brunt of that.' A frown marred his handsome, symmetrical features. 'I'm sorry. I wish you had not ended up as collateral damage. If I could undo it, I would. But, Mia? You are beautiful. Now. Then. Always. I'm sorry that your mother's treatment gave you cause to doubt that, and that my own actions inadvertently—and incorrectly—reinforced her behaviour.'

A tear slid down her cheek as she shook her head, hearing his words but refusing to heed them. Self-preservation was an instinct that died, oh, so hard. But when he kissed her, she let him, and she relaxed into it, because it was just a kiss, it was just sex, it was just physical. Mia's heart was as locked as ever, and Luca's was too. This was safe, this was okay, because they knew when they'd stop seeing each other, and go back to their normal lives. Everything was going to be just fine.

'Mia? How's England?'

Her skin paled as her dad's voice came down the phone line. The lie felt heavy in her gut. But then her eyes drifted across the dazzling white sand beach, following Luca's figure as he ran parallel to the coastline. 'Oh, fine. Yeah, fine.'

'Doing pre-wedding shopping?'

Mia clamped her hands together in her lap. The wedding, which she knew to be inevitable, now loomed as a terrifying drop right off the edge of the earth. Certainty about what she was doing, and why, had begun to recede. She knew the wedding mattered to her parents, the company did too, but what about Mia? She wanted freedom from her parents' oppressive type of love, but was there only one way to obtain that freedom?

'Dad, I wanted to ask you something,' she said without answering. 'Do you have a minute?'

'I have precisely two minutes before my meeting arrives.'

'Great, this won't take long.' The quicker the better in fact, like ripping off a plaster. She furrowed her brow, tummy in knots. 'It's about Luca Cavallaro.'

Silence stretched between them. Saying his name aloud sent a rush of something through Mia—she realised she hadn't done as much since the wedding day.

'Bastard of a man. What about him?'

Mia's cheeks coloured. 'Did you have any

idea, before that day, that he was having... doubts?'

More silence but, this time, Mia was sure she heard it crackle down the phone line. 'What kind of question is that?' Gianni spluttered eventually, either truly indignant or doing an excellent job of feigning it.

'I'm just curious.'

'Mia, as far as I was concerned, the wedding was going to happen.'

She sighed, frustrated. Someone was lying to her, and as she watched Luca running, she knew who she believed. Luca had hurt her, but he was ruthlessly honest. He wouldn't say he'd had a conversation with Gianni if it hadn't taken place. Was it possible her father had misunderstood? Her frown deepened.

'What is all this about, Mia?' Gianni asked sharply. 'That bastard is in the past. Lorenzo is a good man. His family is rich and powerful, the business will be in good hands.'

'As will I?' she asked, ice in her veins. How much of this was about the business, rather than Mia?

'Yes, yes, of course. Now, is that everything?'

CHAPTER SEVEN

WHAT WAS HE DOING? He felt a slip in the side of the road, a precarious tumble, not only likely but almost happening in that moment. Things with Mia were different from anything he'd experienced, different from what he'd anticipated they'd be. She was like a diamond in one of his father's stores, with dazzlingly bright eyes and many, many facets. Every time he thought he understood her, she revealed something else about herself. He didn't think a lifetime would be long enough to properly know her.

But that was for her husband to find out.

Luca tightened his jaw, trying not to think of how that could have been him, if he'd been willing to let the Marini family con him into a worthless business partnership.

He closed his eyes a moment, trying to grab hold of the anchor points in his life, the touchstone moments that informed the man he'd become. The difficulties of his childhood. His mother's poverty despite her hard work—that had taught him a determination to never be hungry again, to never know the discomfort of a winter without electricity. It had taught him a fierce desire to be so rich money became almost inconsequential. His mother's death—sudden and abrupt—and whatever trials he'd had before then had seemed ludicrous, because suddenly the carpet had been ripped from beneath his feet, his whole world tumbled and shattered and unrecognisable without the woman who'd been a bookend to his days for as long as he could remember. She was not a demonstratively loving mother. Perhaps the hurts his father had heaped upon her had closed shut her heart, but, despite a lack of obvious affection, she'd been there for him, even when she was exhausted.

He'd missed her like a limb.

And then, his world had changed again, when a lawyer had arrived in a smart grey suit, with an even fancier grey car, and bundled Luca into the sweet-smelling interior—lollies and air freshener—and taken him to the airport, where he'd boarded a large jet and been flown to the unfamiliar, sticky and hot landscape of Sydney, Australia.

He'd hated his father immediately.

He'd hated him even more when he came to realise that he had a brother just three months older. At twelve, Luca was mature enough to understand what that meant. He'd been conceived while his father's wife was pregnant with Max. His father had cheated—on his mother, and also Max's mother.

Was it any wonder the marriage dissolved? But not simply and quietly, as the word 'dissolved' might have implied. It was a wreck. A total implosion, with sparks and flames and detritus and collateral damage in the form of two young boys who were forced to watch on and listen to it all, who would be shaped for ever by the visage of two grown-ups going out of their way to be as hurtful and angry with one another as they possibly could be.

All of these moments had shaped Luca, had informed his outlook on life, family, relationships. His trust was hard won, but Max had earned it.

Their early relationship had been difficult. Naturally. It didn't help that their father had almost seemed to delight in setting the boys against one another, in fuelling a competition between them. But competition had somehow turned to mutual respect, then to the realisation that they had far more in common than they didn't, and that their differences could, if used in tandem, unite them, strengthen them.

Somewhere along the way, they became a pair.

Except in one vital way: Luca swore he would never touch one cent of the Stone fortune, and he hadn't. To this day, his wealth was a by-product of his own work, his sweat, strength, daring, guile and genius. He'd worked harder than anyone he knew to rise to the top, to prove to his father that he didn't need him. Or perhaps that he shouldn't have ignored him, for the first twelve years of Luca's life. A deeply buried sense of worthlessness, of having been unwanted by his father, was hard to shake, and Luca had learned the best way to conquer that vulnerability was to never need anyone again.

He couldn't be hurt if he stood completely on his own, a pillar of autonomy and strength, a man utterly untouched by concern for another.

But Mia...

He dragged a hand through his hair, eyes blinking open and landing immediately on her, where she lay on the sun lounger, body a deep caramel, hair like gossamer silk so his fingers itched to reach out and touch her.

Mia was not his concern, he reminded himself emphatically. This week was an aberration, a rare moment of indulgence that he'd get out of his system and be done with. He didn't need her. He didn't need anyone.

But that didn't mean he didn't want to fix something inside her that he suspected he'd helped break. Moving quickly, he reached for his phone and placed a couple of calls, a sense of something like pleasure building in his gut as he imagined her reaction, when she realised what he'd done.

'What is all this?' Mia stared at the bags and bags and bags with a knotty feeling in her stomach.

'You didn't have time to pack clothes,' he reminded her, gesturing to the bags as if it were nothing.

But Mia read the labels and knew that the island of things on her bed constituted an investment of tens of thousands of dollars, probably more like hundreds of thousands. Particularly when her eyes alighted on a small burgundy bag at the front with gold swirling writing that said *Stone*. His family's jewellery stores were amongst the most prestigious in the world. And the most expensive.

'Luca…' Her voice faltered as she turned to face him, ambivalence on her delicate features. 'This is too much.'

'It's just fabric.'

That was so like him, to simplify this gesture down to the nuts and bolts.

'I hate shopping,' she said with a shake of her head.

'This isn't shopping. Someone else has done that for you.'

'Who?'

'Does it matter?'

'I'm interested.' She moved to the bags out of idle curiosity, pressing one apart with her fingertips.

'An assistant.'

'You had your assistant buy me clothes?'

'Why not?'

'I just—' She furrowed her brow. 'I'm just confused. I don't understand why you'd do this.'

'Am I not allowed to gift you something?'

'This isn't something. It's many somethings, and it's extravagant and...' She shook her head. 'I don't know. I'll feel strange keeping them after this week.'

His eyes narrowed before his face was quickly wiped of emotion. 'Then don't keep them. Donate them. For now, let me have the pleasure of seeing you try some on.'

It would be ungrateful and churlish to refuse, though Mia also hated trying clothes on. However, she discovered that the clothing Luca's clever assistant had selected was so beautiful that, rather than feeling her usual revulsion at the activity, she actually enjoyed slipping into the silky fabrics, the delicate skirts and bottom-hugging jeans.

'They're beautiful,' she admitted after a third outfit change.

'Not the clothes.' He came towards her, linking his hands behind her waist. 'You are beautiful, Mia.'

Her heart fluttered; this time, she absolutely believed him.

'And now, this one.'

He reached for the burgundy bag and her heart began to thump. 'What is it?'

His smile was knowing as he reached into the bag and removed a small velvet box. 'Something I wanted you to have.'

She bit down on her lip, butterflies bursting through her.

The box shape was all wrong for a ring, and she was glad. A ring from Luca would remind her of the last ring he'd given her. No, she corrected swiftly. He hadn't ever given her a ring. One had been couriered over with the contracts, to Mia's father, who'd given it to Mia unceremoniously, except for a throwaway remark on his having presumed Luca Cavallaro might have sprung for a large diamond.

'A larger diamond would have made your fingers look so much slimmer, Mia. What a shame!' Jennifer had chimed in.

For her part, Mia had loved it. The ring had been small and delicate, a fine gold band with a single gemstone in the centre. Not a diamond, but an emerald, it had caught the light and refracted it into the room.

She'd had it sent back to Luca by her assistant the week after their non-wedding.

She couldn't have borne the thought of having it in her home.

With fingers that weren't quite steady, she opened the box, her breath catching in her throat at the sight of the necklace within. Her father would have been delighted, for surely this necklace was both exquisitely beautiful and also very valuable.

Her finger ran over the chain—platinum gold with a round diamond set in each inch or so, leading to a teardrop diamond with three solitaires on either side. It was incredibly beautiful. Despite the double-digit carats, it was still, somehow, delicate and wearable.

It was far more valuable than anything Mia owned, and yet she could immediately see herself in it.

He'd chosen well.

But perhaps this hadn't been Luca's choice, so much as the clever work of an assistant.

'May I?'

Her lips pulled to one side and she nodded jerkily, turning and catching her hair over one shoulder, stomach swooping as she waited for him to fasten it behind her neck. His fingers brushed her flesh there and she jumped, her cells flooding with awareness and need. She lifted her hand and felt the diamonds, then turned a little so she could catch her reflection in the mirror.

Her breath burned in her lungs.

It wasn't just the necklace. It wasn't just the clothes. It wasn't just the man standing behind her, so rugged and addictively attractive. It was *everything*, a whole combination of these things. It was standing in this room of Luca's house, in a town he'd brought back to life for her, it was seeing herself like this, that made Mia fully realise this was a reality she could have been living.

If the forks in the road of life hadn't driven him away, if, instead, he'd been waiting at the church for her, dressed in a tuxedo and standing up at the front, those dark eyes watching her, waiting for her, she would now be Mrs Luca Cavallaro.

And then what? a voice in the back of her head demanded. You'd be desperate for the children he'd never give you. Desperate for the love he'd never give you.

And she knew then that her innermost doubts were accurate.

If she'd married Luca, she would have fallen

completely head over heels in love with him. If she'd married Luca, she'd have wanted far more than he could ever give her, and Mia's life, despite the trappings, would have been a misery.

All of this was an illusion.

Despite the way he made her feel, despite the happiness spreading through her, threatening to make her forget, Mia knew the most important thing she could do this week was keep a firm hold of reality. Because none of this was real. None of this would exist by the end of the week.

She wanted to keep things casual, to be relaxed and light-hearted, but something was pulling at Mia, a desperate need to understand the one thing that didn't make sense.

'Why?' She met his eyes in the reflection, her heart lurching in a now-familiar response to looking directly at him—and being seen.

'Because it suits you.'

'I mean, why all of this?' Her hand gestured towards the bed. 'You didn't have to—'

'I wanted to.'

'Okay, but why?'

'So many questions.'

'One question, that you haven't answered.'

His lips compressed, showing, momentarily, his impatience, but then he gave a nonchalant shrug and put his hands on her hips, turning her to face him properly. 'Because you deserve this. And because I am sorry. I have spent the last year convinced you were as bad as your parents, that you were as guilty as they, and now—'

'Now?' she whispered.

'I know that's not the case.'

She frowned. 'Why?'

'Another question?'

She nodded once.

'I can tell. I was wrong about you. I treated you badly, and I regret it. Please, accept my apology.'

So the necklace was a guilt gift? She didn't want it to take the shine off things, but it did, even when, on her fateful non-wedding day, she would have given anything for Luca to acknowledge his fault, to actually apologise to her.

'Why do you hate them? Why did you disappear like that?'

'That's more questions,' he said quietly.

'Don't I deserve to know, Luca? It's part of the same history you were so desperate to understand, after all.'

'Perhaps the greater question is how you don't hate them,' he said after a moment. 'The things you've told me about your mother, even the fact they're willing to trade you away with the company…'

'It's really not like that,' she said defensively.

'Isn't it? Why not?'

'The marriage thing is, I know, hard to understand. It's the twenty-first century and I'm in my twenties. It must seem absurd to you.'

He dipped his head. 'I had never heard of something like this, when your father mentioned it.'

'Arranged marriages aren't actually that uncommon,' she said with a lift of her shoulders. 'But nor are they regular. For my parents, this is one of the ways they show love.'

He lifted a brow.

'They worry about me.' She toyed with her fingers. 'They tried to have kids for years. They couldn't. Then, when my parents died—they were old friends—they knew they had to take me, to raise me. I had been sent to foster care, which I hated, and then Jennifer and Gianni appeared and took me in. They loved me so much, when I needed it most.'

He listened silently, but she felt the judgement emanating from him. 'I was only a child and the gratitude I felt to them for saving me from foster care, at a time when I was grieving my parents, made me feel...makes me feel... indebted to them for life.'

'That is not how adoption is meant to work.'

'Perhaps not, but for me, that's how it was. Is. I know they're not perfect,' she said on a sigh.

'And our relationship is complicated. But they do love me, Luca.'

He compressed his lips.

She tried again. 'People aren't just good, or just bad. Good people can make bad decisions, and vice versa, but when you love someone, you have to accept them, all parts of them, and I do. I see them as they are: imperfect, well-meaning people. My parents.' She shrugged again. 'I love them.'

'And if your father has made very bad decisions?'

She narrowed her gaze. 'Has it ever occurred to you that you're wrong about them? That you made a mistake?'

His nostrils flared.

'You've already admitted that you were wrong about me,' she pointed out, gesturing to the bed, laden with gifts. 'So what if you were wrong about them, too?'

So much hung on his acceptance of that.

'I wasn't.'

She shook her head. 'I gather you think Dad lied to you about the company's worth. You've accused him of attempting to scam you. But how can that be? An independent auditor verified the value prior to agreeing to sell it to you. I know my father was very stressed about ensuring all of the financial reports were done accurately.'

'Or perhaps he was stressed for reasons beyond your comprehension?'

She shook her head slowly, wanting to immediately dismiss Luca's insinuation even when she had to acknowledge there was a small possibility she'd misunderstood the behind-the-scenes dealings of her father. After all, Gianni had made a point of keeping Mia away from the financial operations of the business. She was not a signatory on any of the corporate accounts, her role was confined to business development.

'Tell me what you believe he did,' she said quietly, her finger lifting to the largest diamond and pressing to it, remembering the strength and simplicity of gemstones such as this, trying to build that inside her.

He looked torn, as though he wanted to tell her but also didn't. She lifted her hand to his arm, squeezed. 'I'm stronger than you think. I can handle it.'

'I believe you're strong. I just don't know if it's your burden to carry.'

'You don't get to make that determination.'

'With respect, I do.' He took a step backwards, dislodging her hand. 'I know what it's like to lose a parent—I don't mean to death, but to lose respect for them. Your relationship with your father is your own to navigate—and you seem to be doing a good job. You are far better at accepting nuance and imperfection than I am, Mia.'

'But you're keeping something from me that has to do with the company. The value of the company and the sale he's about to make to Lorenzo. Something that will affect my marriage to him?'

A muscle jerked in Luca's jaw. 'It's not my place to get involved, *cara*. Please, leave it at that.'

God, but how he wanted to. He knew he'd done the right thing, to let Mia work it out for herself, to ask questions not of Luca but rather of her father and get the answers that would help her understand why Luca had walked away. And if the old man didn't speak the truth? If he continued to lie to Mia, for the sake of the business deal and the marriage? Desperate people did desperate things and the company's financial status was dire. It was a miracle they'd managed to hobble along throughout this year.

But that didn't mean Luca could be the one to tear it all down for Mia.

How would she feel to realise everything was built on a house of cards? That her father's prosperity was an illusion, that her marriage was destined to fail—at least, that was likely, if Lorenzo was currently blind to the truth of things.

So the alternative was not to tell her. To let her marry a man who might come to resent and hate her, as he would her parents, once he realised that Marini Enterprises was accumulating losses faster than children did sweets.

With a groan, he flicked off the shower, stared at the wall, his body tensed, his mind running three steps ahead. He wanted Mia to be happy. She deserved that. Would Lorenzo be the answer? She seemed to think so. So why did that bother Luca?

He reached for his towel, frustration making his movements brusque.

None of this was his problem.

He was a man who'd sworn off emotional involvement, who was a lone wolf and always would be. What Mia did with her life after this, quite simply, wasn't his concern.

Mia couldn't believe how adept she was becoming at compartmentalising her feelings into different boxes. On the most superficial of levels, the easiest to understand was how Luca made her feel physically. That was a no-brainer. When they were together, they sparked, they buzzed, electricity arced in the air between them and they acted on instinct alone. It was sublime and irresistible.

But when they were apart, for even the smallest amount of time, Mia's thoughts began to spin and twist and turn, and doubts grew, heavy and insistent, so a sense of foreboding was her companion, every minute of those moments, until Luca reappeared and rational, logical thinking was well out of her reach.

'This place is like heaven on earth,' she murmured, on the edge of the pool, staring out at the ocean.

It really was.

But in the back of her mind, there was the beating of a drum, because they'd been here six nights. Tomorrow, they'd leave this paradise, this exemption from reality, and return to Palermo, where her life, her parents, her impending wedding, would all be waiting for her.

And without the answers she desperately wanted.

'I'm glad you like it.'

'I do.' She forced herself to be brave, to confront reality head-on. 'It's hard to believe I won't see it again.' Damn it, her voice cracked ever so slightly.

Was she imagining the way he stiffened at her side? Of course she was. A quick glance at Luca showed him to be the picture of sexy, tousled relaxation. As always, just the sight of him made her pulse thunder. She looked away again quickly.

One more night.

'You can come back any time, *cara*.'

She took the throwaway comment as civility, nothing more. They'd made an agreement that this one week would be the end of their relationship—Mia wasn't going to go back on her word, and she knew he wouldn't either. Too much was at stake to be so foolish.

If she were to back out of her arrangement with Lorenzo, she'd have two failed engagements behind her. And for what? A man who, by his own admission, didn't do serious relationships and didn't want children. And who hated her parents, to boot.

But, that annoying little voice pressured, *isn't it better to be ecstatically happy for a short time than mildly contented for ever?*

And was it really the right thing, to marry Lorenzo? A fortnight ago, she would have said yes, unequivocally, but everything was different now, including Mia, and what Mia wanted from life, and the path forward was no longer a path so much as a mess of sand and grit that she had no concept of how to navigate.

Mia knew two things for certain: she didn't want to consider a life without Luca, but she couldn't consider a life with him in it either. It would never work. So she forced herself to remember that, over and over and over again.

And as the night slipped towards dawn, and their time came close to running out, she had almost convinced herself that she was ready for this. Goodbyes, though, were never easy, even the ones that were utterly necessary.

CHAPTER EIGHT

'HE'S SICK.' LUCA APPRECIATED the fact Max cut right to the chase. And his older brother didn't need to go into further detail. Luca knew that 'he' was their father, and that by 'sick' Max must have meant seriously ill, because he'd have never called in the middle of the night if the old man had a trifling cold. Not that Luca had been sleeping, anyway.

Having dropped Mia at her office earlier that day, he'd found himself ravaged by a vicious, internal war.

On the one hand, he knew there was wisdom in never seeing her again.

It wasn't only wise, it was *right*. Mia had chosen what she wanted in life and her priorities didn't—couldn't—accord with his own.

The fact they hadn't married a year ago was, as it turned out, a blessing in disguise. Why hadn't it occurred to him that the issue of children might prove controversial?

Because he was selfish.

The answer blinked right in front of his eyes, bringing him little pleasure. Her supposition—that children would, at some point, follow marriage—was the more natural of the two.

He knew his strong desire to never put down roots was unusual. How arrogant of him not to have given her any explanation on that score. He hadn't treated her like a person, but, rather, a commodity. He couldn't look back on that time in his life without a deep sense of shame. It was as though he were a different person altogether.

'Luca?'

He drew himself back to the conversation with Max with effort. *'Sì?'*

'He's known for a while.'

Luca grunted. That was so like their father—to conceal something important. 'And?'

'Bottom line? He's probably got weeks, not months.'

Something shifted inside Luca. Though he wasn't close to his father, it was yet another touchstone in his life being eroded away, leaving him with flint in his chest. 'I see.'

'He wants to see you.'

Luca stared at the wall across the room for a long time without speaking. He didn't know what to say. Of course, the norm would have been to immediately assure his brother that he would come home, but Luca hadn't thought of Australia as home for a long time—if ever. It was this foothold of Italy, where his mother had chosen to raise him, where he saw himself in the features of the people he passed on the street and in the rugged landscape that abounded in these parts.

Australia was just where he'd spent his adolescence.

'I'd like to see you, too. There are some things to discuss.'

A sixth sense had the hairs on the back of Luca's neck bristling. 'Oh?'

'I've seen his will.'

Luca moved to his desk chair and sat down, legs wide, elbows braced atop his thighs. 'I don't care about his will.'

'I figured you'd say that.' Max half laughed, but it was a sound without humour.

'And yet you are saying it anyway?'

'Half his business is left to you.'

Luca sat straighter, rubbed his jaw. 'What?'

'Yeah.'

'I told him—'

'I know. But it's your legacy. Look, it's not up to me to speak for the old man, but I wouldn't be surprised if contemplating his own mortality hasn't given him some insight into the past, into things he would change if he could. Maybe it's not enough for you, but I think you'll regret it if you don't come and see him. Listen to him. If you don't like what he has to say, you can leave again.'

'Thank you for your permission,' Luca drawled, then cringed, because Max was his brother, and Luca not only loved him, he respected him, and his opinions. 'I am grateful for your insight,' he tried again, more sincerely. 'But I need to think about it.'

Max was silent and Luca knew him well enough to picture his brother's face, so like his own, with those symmetrical features, angular jaw and chiselled cheekbones. His expression would be one of discontent, but Luca wasn't about to offer more than some consideration.

'Think fast, Luc. I have a bad feeling about this.'

Luca disconnected the call and reached for his Scotch glass in one swift movement, mulling over the news he'd just received, trying to disentangle his feelings from his duties, to weigh up whether he had any duties towards his father or if his father's treatment of the boys, and of Luca's mother, absolved Luca completely. And all the while, Mia's sweetly spoken words ran through his mind. People were neither wholly good nor bad. Had he overlooked the nuance of his father's personality? Good people could make bad decisions, and vice versa.

He let out a gruff noise of frustration.

It wasn't as if he hadn't tried to resolve this.

When he was seventeen, a year before leaving Australia, he'd confronted his dad and given him a chance to offer something, anything, by way of explanation. Apology. Justification. *Anything* that would help Luca understand. But his father had simply shrugged and told him he couldn't change the past and if Luca had an issue with it, that was exactly what it was: Luca's issue. In fact, he'd told his son he needed to toughen up if he ever wanted to amount to anything in this world.

And so the day he turned eighteen, Luca had left, and not looked back.

With each corporate victory, he'd remembered his father's words, the implication that Luca would never be good enough. The biggest delight in his life came from proving his father wrong.

But Luca had also sworn to himself that he'd be different from his father. That he wouldn't make the same mistakes and treat people as expendable. That he wouldn't hurt someone the way his father had hurt his mother, and Max's mother.

So how could he accept what he'd done to

Mia? Who, as it turned out, hadn't deserved even a hint of his anger. Mia, who'd been innocent in every goddamned way.

Luca raked his fingers through his hair, spiking it at odd angles. Suddenly, all he wanted was to see her, to speak to her, to bare his soul to her about his father, to ask her advice. So he poured another Scotch and paced the room, because needing someone was a mistake Luca didn't ever intend to make. Particularly not someone engaged to another man.

'You can't be here.' It was history repeating itself, Luca arriving at her office—though, mercifully, he'd come late in the day again, when most of the staff had left. And her body's response, predictably hectic and flushed, desire pooling between her legs. She was wearing one of the dresses he'd bought for her—as if she could ever donate such a beautiful item that reminded her of him—but now she wished she weren't. It made her feelings for him too obvious.

'I needed to see you.'

Oh, how she needed that too. Her heart lurched and her blood pounded in her veins but she held her ground, standing behind her desk, hoping she looked something like impassive. But how could she? It had been three days since they'd returned from his beach house, and she'd been waiting, hoping, wishing to see him even when she was glad each night that she hadn't weakened.

She was getting married.

Her parents had met with Lorenzo's parents only the day before, for a long, family lunch. The expectation was set. The business merger was happening. Grandchildren were being planned.

Strange how, a few weeks ago, Mia would have said she wanted children more than anything on earth, and now the thought left her strangely hollow. Because when she closed her eyes and imagined swelling with new life, holding her baby in her arms, it was Luca's eyes that stared back at her, a son or daughter of his to love and hold and raise and care for.

'You can't be here,' she repeated, to remind herself of all the reasons this was wrong.

'Why?' He prowled towards her but stopped on the other side of the desk, a strange echo of a time in their lives when their businesses had been destined to merge. Her heart crackled. How different it should have been...

'Because we had an agreement.'

'Agreements can be changed.'

She shook her head angrily—angry with herself for being secretly glad to see him, angry with him for arriving like this and skittling her common sense. 'You promised me.'

'So? I'm breaking it.' Then, with an angry sigh, 'Apparently that is a skill of mine.'

She flinched, because she didn't like to hear him speaking that way about himself, and because she hated the truth of his words. She tried to remind herself that she had also thought she couldn't trust him—wouldn't trust him.

Her heart stammered, because even as she thought that, on a soul-deep level, her trust for him was intrinsic. Perhaps his being here showed why she *could* rely on him.

'I need to see you.'

Need.

Yes, it was need. He needed her as she needed him. But it was lunacy. This thing with Luca had no future, they needed to end it.

'We had a deal,' she reminded him through gritted teeth. And then, as if to remind them both: 'I'm getting married.' She lifted her hand between them, showing the ring she wore, a ring she'd come to feel was unnaturally heavy.

'Don't.' His eyes whipped from the ring to her face, his lips were tight. 'I don't want to talk about your wedding right now.'

She stared at him, completely lost. 'Well, what do you want to talk about?'

He paced away from her then, towards the

office, bracing an arm against the window and staring out at the setting sun.

She took advantage of his distraction to study him, to drink in the sight of him, because she'd been missing him with all of her soul. She was so weary. So exhausted.

It felt to Mia as though she'd boarded an express train to the wrong destination and there was no way to get off it, no way to stop. She'd made a commitment—to Lorenzo, to his family, to her parents. She couldn't back out.

Oh, none of them was pretending this was a romantic connection. They all knew it to be a business deal. But that didn't mean they weren't taking it seriously, that they didn't have their hearts set on the union.

Two powerful, prosperous families uniting was the epitome of her parents' hopes for Mia, and Lorenzo's for him.

'My father is dying.'

It was the last thing she'd expected him to say.

Luca had made an artform of evading her questions.

She knew a little about his family empire—the Stone jewellery stores were famous the world over, so too was the fortune attached to the business, but Luca's own business concerns were distinct, based largely outside Australia, his prosperity his own creation. Luca had never discussed his father or brother with Mia. She pressed her palms to her desk.

'My father is dying,' he repeated, turning back to Mia, frowning, staring at her as if trying to make sense of something she couldn't understand. 'And all I could think, when I heard this news, was that I had to see you. I have spent the last two days fighting the urge to come to you,' he explained with urgency, and she felt it—how hard he'd fought, how annoyed he was that he'd lost that fight. 'I know what we agreed, what I promised. But I need you. I need your help. Is that selfish of me?'

Was it? She didn't know. Needing someone and being able to admit that seemed like a watershed moment, but for what? Mia couldn't answer, she knew only that she felt something forging between them, interlocking, something important, and she knew that she was glad. He needed her, and she wanted to be there for him. His father was dying, and he'd come to her.

Something rose inside her chest and it wasn't until she heard the noise that Mia realised it was a sob.

She smothered her mouth with her hand and came around her desk, striding quickly to Luca and standing in front of him.

'I'm sorry,' she whispered, lifting up onto the tips of her toes and kissing him, salty tears in her mouth as she wrapped her arms around his neck and held herself there, breathing in his scent, hoping that her closeness would give him strength and whatever else it was he needed from her.

'Will you give me tonight?'

'Just tonight?' she asked, softly, pulling back so her eyes could read his face. When would it ever be enough with them? She was drowning in the middle of the ocean, and she wasn't even sure she cared.

Emotions flickered in his eyes and then, to her immense relief, he shook his head once. 'I won't make that promise again.' The words were virtually growled from him. 'Give me tonight, Mia. We'll negotiate what comes next…later.'

Her heart twisted and her stomach churned. She knew the smart thing would be to say no. To tell him he could stay in her office for a while, to talk to her from a safe distance, but that then he should go, and let her go, and that would be the end of it.

But Luca was standing there with his heart on his sleeve—a heart she hadn't really even known he possessed—and Mia couldn't walk away from this. Danger swirled all around her. She knew what she was jeopardising, and she knew that Luca would never be what she wanted long term, but right now, in this moment, he was her everything, and she couldn't step away from that.

'Yes,' she said quietly, terrified. 'But you must leave now. Go. I'll follow when I can.'

His expression was impossible to interpret. Relief, but there was something else too, like a whip, that cracked between them.

'I can wait for you.'

'No.' She was adamant. 'We can't leave here together, and you know it. You shouldn't come here. You can't come here again.' She pressed a finger to his lips, silencing whatever response he might have been poised to make. 'I'm glad you reached out to me, though.' She lifted onto her tiptoes and replaced her finger with her mouth, just a light quick kiss, a down payment of what would come next.

He stalked out of her office with a face like thunder, head bent, moving quickly towards the narrow bank of elevators, almost willing her father to appear, to see him, to speculate and wonder. Selfishly, he wanted that. To throw the cat well amongst the pigeons and leave them in no doubt of what was going on. Of how much he wanted Mia after all. Of the fact she was *his*. Clearly that explained why he had come here not once, but twice. On some level, he welcomed discovery. In the hopes it would lead to the cancellation of her wedding? And then what?

Frustration gnawed at his gut. How could she go through with this? Mia was too beautiful and full of love to enter into a marriage of convenience. A business deal, and nothing more. And when he thought of another man calling himself Mia's husband, touching her, making love to her, Luca felt as though a vein in his head might explode.

Yes, he welcomed the idea of discovery, but for Mia's sake, he was as incognito as possible anyway, because he knew she'd be devastated if anyone found out about them. Fate smiled upon her, and the lift doors opened immediately, shepherding him away from the risk of discovery, for now.

Mia arrived at his home an hour later and slipped in the front door with the key he'd given her. Having a key to his place did something strange to her belly. As she inserted it into the lock, she had the weirdest sense of coming home, of truly coming home, and again she felt that jarring fantasy take over—what it would have been like if they were married, this were their house and she were simply coming back from a day's work.

The clawing feeling of tears made her throat

ache. How could she yearn so much for something she'd never known? But then, tonight wasn't about her, and their failed engagement. Luca needed Mia. He'd come to her because he needed her help, and she would give him that.

Mia took a moment, composed herself, then stepped fully inside, closing the door and stepping deeper into his home. The lights were dimmed, and he'd lit candles—long tapered ones that had been burning for long enough that wax had formed streaky puddles down their sides and onto the base of the candle holders. Soft, jazzy music played. She sighed as she entered his lounge room fully, looking around, eyes landing on Luca at the grand piano, head bent, fingers pressed to the keys without any noise coming out.

She padded over to him silently and wrapped her arms around him from behind, pressed her head to his shoulder and just held him, hoping, as she had in her office, that some physical strength and certainty would pass from her to him with that small gesture.

They stayed like that for a long time, just the softly shifting glow of candles to alert them to the passage of time, but eventually, Mia stood, then came to sit beside him on the stool.

'Do you play?' he asked, turning to face her,

eyes roaming her face almost as if he'd never seen her before.

She shook her head. 'I took lessons for a few years but "Three Blind Mice" is about all I remember.'

One side of his lips lifted in soft acknowledgement of that.

'And you?'

A muscle jerked in his jaw. 'My mother taught me.'

'I didn't realise that.' Then again, why would she?

'She learned as a little girl. She was very good. She lost a lot over the course of her lifetime—her parents threw her out when they discovered she was pregnant with me and, after that, her life was hardly comfortable. She moved down here, to Sicily, where she had a cousin she was close to. She got my mother a job, and I believe they treated her well.' His voice showed restrained anger. 'At the hotel she worked at, there was a piano in the lobby. The manager would let her play, early in the mornings, before it got busy. So a few times a week, she would take me in to learn as well.' He pressed his fingers lightly to the keys. 'She was a hard teacher.'

Mia's smile was soft, involuntary. 'In what way?'

'Completely intolerant of mistakes, even

when I was a beginner. My mother spoke music like a second language. It just came naturally to her. She found my errors jarring. We couldn't afford a piano, but one day, our neighbours had a piece of furniture delivered and I saved the box it came in. I measured out the pieces with a black pencil and drew a keyboard on top, so that I could practise finger placement at home.'

Mia's heart flipped over at the very idea of the earnest little boy he'd been. 'You wanted to make your mother proud.'

He dipped his head once in what Mia took to be silent acknowledgement of that. 'I was fascinated by the piano, and the way she could coax such beautiful music out of something otherwise inanimate. I wanted to speak the language too.'

'Show me.'

His gaze locked to hers, the air between them sparking and growing warm, so Mia felt the hairs on her arms lift and the cells in her body tingle. Then, he turned away, so his face was in profile, and his hands pressed to the keys, picking up in time with the music that was playing, echoing it perfectly, so it was a form of surround sound, but so much better, because when Luca played, he added a richness and emotion to the music that Mia hadn't been aware of before. His fingers moved skilfully and fast over the keyboard. She watched them for a few moments but then his face drew her attention back, because it was so fascinating, lost in concentration not, she suspected, on the piece he was playing, but rather on the situation with his father. She wriggled closer, because suddenly it wasn't enough to sit beside him, she wanted to feel him, to touch him, and to know he could also feel her.

He pulled his fingers away from the piano. The song had ended. But another song picked up, on the album he was playing—this time, Luca didn't accompany it.

Shifting a little, he turned to face her.

'She must have been thrilled with how well you learned.'

His brows flexed. 'My mother was not given to lavish praise,' he said with a hint of humour that Mia took for deflection. How that must have hurt a young boy who'd worked so hard to impress her.

'You play beautifully,' she said. Surely he knew that. He didn't need Mia to tell him. But it was possible Luca had never been told before, and she couldn't bear the thought of that.

It was such a strange thought, a silly aberration. As if Luca lacked self-esteem! He was naturally the best and the brightest, a king amongst men, the kind of person who could walk into any room and take control. He didn't need Mia praising his piano-playing abilities, of all things.

'How old were you when she died?' Mia prompted. In the past, he'd evaded her questions, but tonight, he'd come to her, acknowledging that he needed help, and something vital had shifted between them. Mia didn't understand it, but she felt the rhythms of their relationship shift and wasn't afraid this time that he might not answer.

He pressed his fingers to the keys; the noise now a little jarring. 'Twelve.'

She shook her head sadly. 'Still just a boy.'

'I didn't feel it.' He put a hand on her thigh, staring down at his tanned fingers against the silk fabric of the dress he'd bought her. 'She died and I was alone. I'd known, all my life, that my father wasn't a part of our life. He didn't want me. He didn't want her.' His jaw tightened.

'And had she wanted him?' Mia pushed softly.

'She never really spoke about their relationship.' Then, a heavy, angry exhalation of breath. 'But yes. She was in love with him. Even after the way he treated her, she loved him—I could tell. And I hated her for that, but I hated him more.'

'Why would you hate her?' Mia pushed, surprised.

'What a weakness! To love and want a person who rejected you as he had her. I hated the power she gave to him, the way she worshipped him even when he'd thrown her life into such abject poverty.'

'When he'd refused to acknowledge you,' Mia murmured, because naturally a child would take that view, would feel hurt and rejected, and would want their mother to share that viewpoint.

'I never knew him. But she did. She knew and loved him and pined for him. She let him ruin her life. I saw how vulnerable and weak that love made her.'

'And swore you'd never be in that position,' she murmured, feeling as though a door had opened, showing her a side of Luca that was important and vital, a door that helped her understand who he was.

His eyes seemed to pierce Mia's soul. 'No one should be in that position.'

Her lips tilted to the side. 'Your mother was unlucky to fall in love with someone who didn't love her back.' Something clanged inside Mia. A realisation, or a slow-spreading dawn, but she couldn't quite see her way to understanding it. She knew only that something was shifting, that she was shifting and changing.

'Tell me about your father.' She pressed her

fingers to the keys lightly, her lips bending into a half-smile. 'You don't talk about him at all.'

'No.' His Adam's apple shifted.

'Why not?'

'My mother had an expression. If you cannot say anything nice—'

'Don't say anything at all.' She moved her hand to his, lacing their fingers together. The music in the background was slow, gentle. It threaded through Mia, pulling at her emotions. 'Is there nothing nice you can say about him?'

'He's a competent businessman.'

She arched a brow, her smile involuntary, softened with disbelief. 'Competent?'

'Not brilliant.'

'Not brilliant like you?'

Luca's nostrils flared. 'Perhaps not as motivated as I am. Being born into immense wealth has that effect on people, in my experience.'

'Your brother?'

Luca considered that. 'Max is different. We are half-brothers, but so alike, though he feels more of a connection to the Stone family businesses. He grew up knowing, from birth, that it was his destiny to inherit them, to take over from our father. Our grandfather drilled that into him from a young age. Max had little choice.'

'Do you think he might have chosen to do something else?'

'Who can say?' Luca lifted his shoulders. 'I believe he's happy. He oversees the pearl-farming operations.'

'What a fascinating thing to do.' Mia shook her head. 'I mean, of course I know pearls come from the sea, but I never really think of them being farmed, growing, being harvested.'

'It's an impressive process.' He was quiet. She wondered if he was thinking what she was: that she'd have loved to see the pearl farm. With him.

'You weren't interested in moving into that line of work?'

'No.'

'Luca, why don't you use their last name?'

'I was a Cavallaro first. I lost my mother, there was no way I'd give away her name.'

Mia could understand that. 'Did it bother your father?'

His smile was bitter. 'Immensely. In fact, he would often introduce me as Luca Stone. I corrected him, every time.'

Mia could imagine the determined teenager he'd been. She pressed her cheek to his shoulder, resting her head there, enjoying his nearness and warmth.

'When did you last see your father?'

'He flew to Rome for my twenty-first birthday.'

Mia shook her head sadly. 'So long ago. Did something happen?'

Luca lifted a hand, cupping her cheek. 'Why? Do you want to fix it, Mia?'

She frowned, hating how easily he understood her. 'You asked me for help,' she couldn't help reminding him.

'So I did.'

'Was that not in the hope I could fix this?'

'I'm a pragmatist. Some things are beyond fixing.'

'But not beyond trying.' She tilted her face into his hand, her heart swelling and squeezing. 'You fixed me, Luca. You fixed what you did, with our wedding.'

His eyes swept shut a moment, as if her words were too hard to fathom.

'You have a more forgiving temperament than I do, remember? You see the good in people, even through their faults.' He pressed a hand to her chest. 'You are a beautiful woman, with the kindest heart in the world.'

Mia swallowed past a lump in her throat, but she wouldn't let the praise—no matter how ground-breaking—distract her from this conversation. 'Tell me what he did, Luca. Tell me why you can't forgive him.'

CHAPTER NINE

MIA HAD ALWAYS loved mornings. As corny as it sounded, there was something exciting about the breaking of a fresh day, filled with promise and newness, of memories not yet made. She'd been a firm subscriber to the belief that all things looked better with the dawn.

But this morning, when she woke, it was with a strange heaviness in her chest, a sense of dread that she couldn't immediately comprehend.

And then she remembered. Her fantasy. Her secret game of make-believe, that this was all real. That waking up in Luca's bed was normal. That he was really hers, not in this mad, passionate, temporary way, but in a forever and ever kind of way.

She stared across his room at the light breaking through in a fine beam and her stomach dropped to her toes.

It wasn't real, and she needed to go.

But how could she leave him?

Memories of last night played through her mind. She shifted a little, rolling over so she could see him. His beautiful face, so fascinating and strong, so filled with detail and emotion, restful now, in contrast to how he'd been last night, when he'd told her, in short, unwilling snatches at first, and then longer, reflective monologues, about his life.

His whole life.

His upbringing. The mother he loved and respected but had never felt a warm affectionate love from. The shock of her death. The resilience he'd showed in facing that head-on. The courage in moving to Australia. The despair at breaking up a family, of knowing himself—indirectly—to be the cause of it. His very existence was the death knell to his father's marriage and his brother's family.

As for his father, Mia knew she shouldn't stand in judgement of someone she'd never met, but it was natural to have developed a dislike for the man who'd treated Luca so badly. Oh, Luca didn't say as much. He spoke sparingly, the details given almost unwillingly, but he'd said enough for Mia to glean a pretty clear picture.

She understood Luca so much better now.

And that was dangerous, because understanding him brought her two steps closer to forgiveness, to true forgiveness, and, without the resentment that she'd become used to, she was terrified of what her feelings might morph into. Suddenly, the simplicity of her life, her future, the plans she'd calmly laid in place for everything she wanted seemed like a house of cards.

Her marriage to Lorenzo was the smart choice. Maybe it wasn't even really a choice any more? Plans were in motion, guests had been invited, her parents were excited. And, more importantly, the business contracts were being signed, the merger too important to her parents to jeopardise.

For every answer she'd received last night, dozens of questions proliferated through her now, as she looked at her future with the exact opposite of clarity. She could barely see two steps in front of herself, but when she thought of marrying Lorenzo, she felt only a deep, terrifying sense of panic.

And yet, at the same time, she had to acknowledge that whatever feelings she had for Luca, he would never be her future.

He was a lone wolf. Not born that way, but shaped into it by life, and by a self-preservation mechanism that meant he wouldn't change easily.

Even for her?

She heard the question and squeezed her eyes shut against the dangerous bloom of hope.

This couldn't go on.

They couldn't keep doing this.

Because Mia wasn't an automaton. When she'd first met Luca, there'd been the most overwhelming sense of recognition, as if, here he was, the person she hadn't even known she'd been waiting for all her life. She'd dismissed those feelings then as a stupid infatuation—he was beautiful and she was totally inexperienced and in awe of his larger-than-life charisma.

She knew him now. She was no longer mesmerised nor intimidated by him. But the sense that he was a complementary part of her wouldn't shift. With a growing surge of panic, because everything was getting way too out of hand, she crept carefully from his bed and tiptoed out of the room, taking one last peek at his sleeping frame, closing her eyes and trying to steel herself against the gargantuan task ahead.

In his kitchen, she found a notepad and ran her finger over the top—the embossed logo for his company. Even that made her heart beat faster, and love squeezed her insides into a different shape. Because it *was* love.

Love for him, his personality, temperament, his strength, determination, intelligence, all the parts of him. Just as he'd said. She loved. Her heart was his. She saw his complexity, his perfections and failings, and loved *all* of them.

'Oh, God,' she groaned softly, picking up a pen and writing quickly, ignoring the tears that were threatening.

Dear Luca,
I hope last night helped. I think you know, deep down, what you need to do.
    I'll be thinking of you in Australia, wishing you all the best.
Goodbye.
Love, Mia

She signed it with love because it was true, and because, though she'd never be stupid enough to tell him how she felt, nor to place that burden upon him, it felt like a small victory, a cheating, to be able to put in writing the honesty of her feelings.

But the 'goodbye' above it almost hurt her to write.

She stepped out onto the kerb in the early morning sunshine and walked quickly to her car, head bent, determined not to look back. A single glance, a moment's pause, and she'd lose her will. She had to do this—there was no alternative.

She didn't consciously make the decision then and there, but by the time Mia arrived at her office, it was with the grim understanding that she absolutely could not marry Lorenzo di Angelo. In fact, she was appalled that she'd ever agreed to go along with the plan. It was as though loving Luca had woken her up to what she deserved in life, to what she'd be denying herself in marrying someone she barely knew and didn't love, didn't desire. And she was asking Lorenzo to make the same sacrifice, all for the sake of their family businesses! What a silly, short-sighted decision to make.

Though that explanation gave the thought process a veneer of rationality that wasn't really behind Mia's decision. The truth was, when she thought of marrying Lorenzo, of marrying anyone other than Luca, she felt a visceral, stomach-rolling sense of despair.

There were many times in Mia's life when she'd ignored her instincts and deferred to her parents, but this was not a time for that. She would not marry Lorenzo di Angelo, no matter how embarrassing it was to extricate herself from the situation now. She'd been able to go along with it, just, when she'd thought things with Luca were meaningless and purely physical—though had she ever really believed that? But now that she understood her heart, it would be wrong on every level to marry Lorenzo.

With the decision made, she walked past her own office door and approached her father's.

Her stomach looping in knots as she braced for what was going to be one of the most difficult conversations of her life. She loved Luca Cavallaro, and while she wasn't foolish enough to hope he might love her back, nor that there was any future for her, that love still deserved better than for Mia's marriage to another man. And with that in mind, she held Luca in her heart like a talisman, a strength she needed more than anything in this moment.

'Do you have a second to talk?'

Gianni was staring at his computer screen, a frown etched into his face, so Mia's own lips tilted downwards. He slammed the laptop shut, gestured to his seat. 'Of course. What is it?'

Mia's stomach rolled. Now that she'd reached the moment of truth, she struggled to know exactly how to say what she wanted to say. 'It's about Lorenzo.'

His eyes narrowed imperceptibly. 'Is something wrong? Has he contacted you?'

Mia shook her head. 'No. No. Nothing like that. I mean, yes. Something is wrong.' She made a sound of exasperation, stood up, paced towards the windows and tried to take solace from the familiar view. 'I can't go through with it.'

Gianni jackknifed out of his chair. 'What?'

'The wedding.' She twisted her fingers together. 'I need to cancel it. I can't marry him.' She felt as though she were suffocating. 'I don't love him. I'll never love him. I can't marry him.'

'I don't believe this. You are supposed to be getting married in a matter of weeks…'

'I know. It's not ideal. I know I promised him, you, his family. I get it. I'm letting everyone down. But I can't go through with it. I'm sorry.'

'Sorry?' he repeated, dragging a hand through his hair. 'Mia, I don't think you understand what you're saying.'

'But I do. For the first time in a long time, I understand myself, my words, my wants, perfectly. I will not marry Lorenzo di Angelo. The company will have to be sold without the marriage as a part of the deal.'

Gianni's face drained of all colour. 'It's not possible.'

'Of course it's possible,' she said firmly, refusing to allow her resolve to be weakened. 'Companies change hands every day without some feudal marriage deal.'

'This is different.'

'Why? Because I'm me? Why do you think I need to marry Lorenzo di Angelo? Do you honestly not think I can stand on my own two feet?'

He stared at her, eyes boring through her, then collapsed back in his chair, as though the weight of the world were pressing down on him.

'I need you to marry him, *principessa*.'

The childhood name was like an arrow through Mia's heart. She walked slowly across the room, alarm bells blaring now. Her father was crumpled; destroyed.

'What is it?' she asked, the tone of her voice carefully wiped of her anxieties. But she *knew* that he'd been lying to her. She knew that Luca had told the truth. Even when he'd been careful not to tell her too much, he'd said enough for Mia to understand that her father's business was in a bad way.

'Oh, God,' she whispered, coming to crouch at his side. 'Tell me the truth, Dad. Tell me everything: how bad is it?'

It was bad.

As her father finally, slowly, spelled out the truth: that the business had been running on air for eighteen months—which was the sole reason he'd looked for a buyer in the first place—Mia realised just how heavy his burden had been. But the older man had looked for solutions in all the worst ways.

'Do you have any idea what you've done?' she asked, lifting fingers to her lips, numb from the revelation she'd just listened to.

'I had no choice!'

She shook her head. 'This is *illegal*, Dad. You

cannot falsify corporate figures for the purpose of enticing someone to buy the company. You cannot seriously have thought this wouldn't be found out?'

'But by then, you would be married, perhaps even pregnant. They would not be able to press charges.'

'Of course they could have. It would have been a sham marriage, not a real one. There's no love between Lorenzo and me!'

'It is still a marriage,' he insisted.

'So I would have been, what? Insurance? You've turned me into an accomplice.' She thought of the guilt Luca had laid at her feet when he'd learned the truth, naturally presuming she was a part of the deception. 'Damn it, Dad, you've made me guilty by association.'

'But you are not. And anyone who knows you will see that.'

'You cannot do this.'

'Nor can I let the company go, our family fall into bankruptcy.'

'Is it really so bad?' She shook her head. 'It can't be. I'd *know*.'

'I have been able to make things work—just barely—but it's all borrowed, Mia. Everything. My debts are—profound.'

Her heart shattered. 'Oh, Papa.' Tears filled her eyes then and she hugged her dad. Nothing mattered more than helping him find a way through this. Judgement was irrelevant. 'This is what Luca knew, isn't it? It's why he walked out on the wedding.'

Gianni's eyes were like flint for a moment and then he slumped forward. 'Yes. He knew. I don't know how…'

Mia let out a deranged half-laugh. 'Because he's ridiculously intelligent and thorough. He came to you about this, didn't he?'

Gianni nodded and Mia felt as though she'd been stabbed through the heart. She'd known one man was lying to her, but not both. They'd both known the truth, all this time, and neither had loved nor respected her enough to be honest. She pressed her fingernails into her palm, heart stammering. 'So a week before the wedding, you knew he wouldn't go through with it—'

'I thought he still would. I honestly believed—'

'No, you hoped,' she contradicted fiercely. 'Because you were desperate. You threw me to the wolves rather than face the reality of the situation. You let him do that to me.'

'When I didn't hear from him again, I presumed he had calmed down. I knew how much he wanted the business…'

'Not enough,' she whispered, 'to tie himself

to our family after such a blatant deception.' She squeezed her eyes shut, because her world was crumbling down around her shoulders and Mia didn't want to bear witness to that destruction.

A million emotions throttled through Mia as she left the office that night. Anger, disbelief, incredulity, panic and despair. She felt a million things and sought refuge in one emotion that was satisfying and for which there was an easy outlet.

Anger.

Anger at Luca.

Who *had* known the truth, and refused to tell her, time and time again, even when she'd begged him. And he'd tried to make that sound noble!

Anger at the man who'd made love to her, who'd treated her so gently, who'd acted as though he were protecting her by keeping this secret, rather than taking the coward's way out, and all the benevolent, loving feelings he'd stirred the night before evaporated, leaving only waspish rage in their place.

Perhaps it wasn't fair to blame Luca. What did he owe her, after all? But the fact of the matter was that her love made her want more from him, made her expect more of him, and he'd failed her. It hurt. It hurt more than his abandonment on their wedding day ever had, because she *loved* him, and he'd let her down. He had left her to fail, rather than being with her, united, a team.

A sob was wrenched from Mia's chest. They *weren't* a team. They never would be.

Rather than give into the desperate sadness that realisation brought, she focused on her anger—a safe emotion, one that would serve her well.

Before she'd even realised what she was doing, Mia had started the engine of her little red Fiat and was turning it away from her home and, instead, towards Luca's, her ears roaring with the sound of her thundering blood the whole drive, so she heard nothing and saw almost as little.

Relief flooded him when she arrived. This was not the first time she'd asked him to leave her alone, but it was the first time he'd truly intended to at least try to listen. It was the only thing he could do. They both knew there was no future here.

But when Mia arrived at his front door and used the key she still possessed to let herself in, an unfamiliar emotion surged in his chest. He wanted to run to her, to wrap his arms around her, to laugh with giddy relief because he'd *missed* her, but he did none of those things.

He was Luca Cavallaro, a man of no emotions, and he wouldn't further complicate the situation by doing anything that might undermine that opinion of him.

'Damn you,' she said quietly, slamming the door then holding her ground, shaking all over, like a beautiful, delicate leaf. 'Damn you to hell, Luca Cavallaro, I hate you. I really, really hate you.'

It was the last thing he expected her to say.

He was glad then that he hadn't moved to her, because it was easier, somehow, to maintain a neutral expression when he was across the room, to conceal the surprise and, yes, hurt— a feeling he didn't know he was capable of— flooding his body, by standing completely still, hands in pockets, eyes fixed on her. Then again, when he'd read that note this morning, hadn't he hated her too? Just a little? For leaving him, for mentioning her marriage, for not being there when he woke up after the night they'd shared, the things he'd told her?

Rage emanated from her frame like waves vibrating through the room. 'I do not know what has happened, but I suggest you tell me why you are so upset.'

'Seriously?'

He waited, watching her, with the strangest feeling in the pit of his stomach. It was as if they were one person. Whatever Mia was feeling, Luca felt too. His insides churned while he stood, impatient but not rushing her.

Mia sucked in a deep breath, her eyes spitting fire. 'You *knew*.'

The penny dropped but before he could speak, Mia continued.

'You knew what he was going through and you didn't tell me. You knew how bad it was, and you said *nothing*, even when you had the opportunity, even when I begged you. How dare you keep this from me? After everything, *everything*, we've shared?'

Her words landed with a thud against his chest but he refused to let her accusation stand. He could see her anger, acknowledge her grief, but he wouldn't take the blame for that. While he hated the idea of Mia thinking the worst of him, the businesslike part of Luca's brain took control, calmly wading through her accusation to find a logical thread. 'These are your father's errors, not mine.'

'How can you be so callous? How can you stand there and apportion blame?'

'Isn't that what you are doing?' Why was he allowing them to argue? It was clear that Mia was upset, that she was spoiling for a fight, but why was Luca fanning the flames of her anger? Why didn't he go to her to offer comfort? Why did he allow her to glare at him and simply stare back, as if his heart were cold, his emotions incapable of being stirred even now, when the opposite was true?

'With good reason,' she roared, stalking towards him then stopping, turning around, shaking her head. 'You are to blame.'

'For your father's ineptitude and dishonesty? Really? How so?'

She spun back, eyes wild, fury unleashed—and hell, he deserved that. It was an utterly insensitive thing to have said. But he was angry—and for no reason he could easily identify, so he sought refuge in the kind of wide-nozzle spray of anger that was immediately satisfying, even if he feared it would turn out to be a mistake.

'Are you mocking him?'

He had—finally—the good sense to slam his lips together.

'You are a pig!' She thrust her hands onto her hips, standing right there, feet wide apart, body tense, ready to fight.

'How could you keep this from me?' she demanded again, lips white-rimmed.

'Your father should have told you. It is him you are angry with, not me.'

'I'm angry with him, yes, but I'm angrier with you.'

Something buzzed in the back of his brain. A realisation. An understanding. But it flitted away again as quickly as it had appeared.

'Do you have any idea what he's done? This is very likely criminal, Luca. As in, illegal. If Lorenzo's parents were to find out, and decided to press charges, not only would he be ruined, he'd go to jail. I could go to jail too, if they suspect, as you did, that I'm involved in this. How could you know this, and not tell me?'

The bottom of his world fell away in a spectacular fashion and an awful heat began to burn Luca's insides. He hadn't even contemplated, for one second, that Mia would pay the price for her father's crimes. But she was right. He'd easily jumped to the conclusion that she was a part of the deception. What if a court thought the same thing? Evidence might exonerate her, but not necessarily. It was easy to allude to a person's involvement and raise a conviction against the odds.

His hands shook. His control was slipping. He turned away from her on the pretence of getting a drink from the bar. A Scotch. God knew he needed it. He threw it back in one harsh motion, then turned to her, slowly, focusing all of himself on containing his emotions.

'I will not allow that to happen.'

'You think you have the power to stop it? You think you're some kind of god?'

A tear slid from the corner of her eye and he stared at her, unable to look away, even when the sight of her was tearing him into pieces.

'It's all so misguided,' she groaned with a shake of her head. 'I cannot understand what he was thinking. It's like the stress temporarily deprived him of sanity. Do you think that might work in his favour? Luca, he's a good man. You have to believe me, this isn't like him.' Tears were falling freely now, and his body physically ached with the need to cross his living room and pull her into his arms.

God, but he wanted her. All parts of her. He wanted Mia for himself. He didn't know how long he'd feel this way, but he wasn't ready to walk away from her, and she clearly still needed him, if even just to sort this out.

And out of nowhere, like the most perfect blade of lightning, Luca saw it. A solution.

An answer to his problems, and to Mia's too. 'I can fix this.'

'You can't,' she sobbed. 'It's gone too far. Oh, why didn't he tell me?'

Luca didn't have time to analyse his idea. He was used to acting on instinct, to taking gambles that almost always paid off, and that had emboldened him, so even when he acknowledged this was a risk, he didn't feel overly worried, because there was, finally, light at the end of the tunnel.

There were limits to what he and Mia could be. They wanted different things. Mia deserved better than him long term. But in the short term, their common goals could be met.

'Agree to be mine, and I will fix everything, Mia.'

She shook her head again. 'I don't understand.'

A strange lurching sensation tipped through him. He ignored it. 'Yes, you do. Agree to stay here with me. Do not marry Lorenzo. Forget about him. Be mine, and I will fix this.'

She bit down on her lower lip, eyes huge in that face that haunted his dreams. He felt euphoric. Victory was within reach. Here was a way to have Mia in his life, his bed, without the guilt, the ticking time bomb of a countdown to her wedding, without the need for secrecy and the hovering certainty that within weeks she'd become someone else's wife. She would be his.

'Your father's business is in a parlous state, but I spent twelve months looking at strategies to strengthen it, twelve months understanding it, inside and out. I will honour the original terms of our deal and become his partner.'

'Do you mean—are you saying you want to marry me?'

It was like a grenade blowing up in his face. Strange that before, when their marriage had simply been part of a business deal, he'd been able to blithely accept the necessity of the albeit odd term of the contracts. But now that he knew Mia so well, now that he'd made love to her over and over, marriage was utterly unimaginable.

Before, there'd been no feelings, and so the idea of a businesslike arrangement had been entirely feasible. Now, it would never be the case. His emotions were dangerously close to the surface with her.

There could be no marriage.

'No. I'm not suggesting we marry, only that you call off your wedding to Lorenzo.' He spoke pragmatically, with no concept of how the words affected her. If he'd been paying attention, he might have seen the way she shrank down into herself, but Luca was fixated on the nearing victory. He could make everything okay for her— and they could get what they wanted too: more time together.

'There's no need for us to do anything stupid. We're adults, it's the twenty-first century, and I'm telling you now, I will bail out your father. I will pay off his debts, ensure the company remains liquid and then set about rebuilding it fully. God knows I need a challenge, particularly now. It's partly what attracted me to the purchase in the first place. I can see the potential in Marini Enterprises, just as my father did before me.'

She flinched, and that, finally, he did see.

But she nodded, slowly. By way of acceptance?

'And I would stay here, with you.'

'Yes.' He breathed out, relief making his body feel light, his feet barely on the ground.

'Until?'

A hard note entered her voice.

'I don't have a crystal ball. Until we agree it's no longer working.'

'How lovely and simple,' she murmured, wrapping her arms across her chest, the phrase at odds with the tension in her body.

He began to tread with care, aware that perhaps victory was not so assured as he was hoping. 'Every bit as simple—if not more so—than our marriage would have been.'

'But you're missing one important thing,' she said, eyes narrowing as they met his.

'I don't believe I am.' He ignored the blinking light in the back of his brain. 'You want to keep seeing me, yes?' He didn't wait for an answer. 'And your father needs to be bailed out, or it's likely he'll face charges in the future. So? Stay here with me, terminate your engagement and I will immediately release the funds needed for his business to remain solvent.'

Her tears began to fall again. Tears of relief? Not joy, he noted, going by the stern pull of her lips.

'I don't want to stay with you like that.'

He stood very still. There were rejoinders at the forefront of his mind, but he didn't speak them. It was better to let her speak, so he would have an idea of how to reply. Because he would win her over. He would convince her this was for the best. Luca knew it would work out—he could have his cake, and eat it, too. Unlike his father, he would be completely upfront with what he wanted, what he expected and how much of himself he was willing to give. Mia wouldn't be hurt the way his mother was hurt, because he was being completely transparent.

'What you're offering isn't enough.'

Her words hit him like a sledgehammer. It was the fear at the very heart of his worst fears, the core damage inflicted on him by a lifetime of having been let down by those he dared let himself love—and hope to be loved back by.

He wasn't enough.

He'd offered her more than he'd ever offered another woman, and it wasn't enough.

'And yet *he's* enough?'

She tilted her chin, glaring at him. 'Lorenzo has nothing to do with this.'

'How can you say that? He's your alternative, isn't he? You want to marry him and just hope for the best?' He couldn't help himself now. He stalked towards her, his hands wrapping around her arms, drawing her to his chest. 'To go to bed with him and pray you conceive a baby, so that he's less likely to prosecute your father? Is that really what you want with your life, Mia?'

'Damn you,' she shouted, lifting her palm and slapping it to his chest. 'Goddamn it, none of this is what I wanted. None of it. To feel this way about you, to have let myself get involved with you, it's all wrong. Everything is wrong.'

'No, it's not,' he responded quickly, moving his body, trapping her between his large, strong frame and the flat, white wall. 'You know that staying is right. You want to hate me for suggesting it, you want to hate me for the offer, but, deep down, you know it's the answer. At least I'm being honest with you. I'm telling you how I feel, what I want, so you don't expect more from me.'

He let his explanation sink in, then pushed another point. 'You don't really want to marry him, and you don't want to stop seeing me. So stay. I'm giving you the perfect solution. You just have to say yes, and I will do everything else, *cara.*'

She was silent and he fervently hoped that was a good sign.

She simply stared up at him, her expression unreadable, save for the grief in her eyes.

'You are mine, Mia. All mine. Do you understand?' And he kissed her, with the furious, passionate possession that was exploding inside his veins.

CHAPTER TEN

IN THEORY, ONE PERSON couldn't belong to another. Mia knew that to be the case. And yet, on the other hand, hadn't she been Luca's from almost the first moment they'd met?

His demanding, hotly asked question rang through her ears and she ached, yearned to agree, to submit to him, but rational thought was like a tentacle wrapped around her brain, pulsing and refusing to quit, so she knew she couldn't subjugate herself to him like this. For money.

And if he'd cared about her at all, if he'd felt even a brief shadow of anything remotely like love for her, he wouldn't have dared suggest it.

Luca didn't do love, though.

He did business and power plays and acquisitions and, ultimately, fierce self-preservation, which meant refusing to love with his dying breath, because love equalled vulnerability. Mia had become just another commodity to acquire, for as long as it suited him to possess her, at which point he'd let her leave, like some stock he no longer had any use for.

And Mia would be damaged.

Beyond repair.

Because every day with Luca, every day of his holding her and saying things like 'you're mine', would make her heart more and more in lockstep with his, would make her forget the temporary nature of what they were doing, would make her want so much more than he could give.

And what of children?

Even if there were the slightest possibility Luca might one day care for her enough to ask her to be his not for a small window of time but for ever, it was impossible to imagine him changing his mind about children.

He'd been adamant, irrefutably absolute.

'I can't,' she whispered, groaning, because just standing like this was drugging her, making her forget all the sensible reasons she'd mentally enumerated.

'Yes, you can. I will fix this, Mia. I will fix this.'

If you stay.

She heard the condition, even though he didn't say it again.

It was her fault. She'd told him, just last night,

that he'd fixed her, had suggested he could fix anything, and it had gone to his head, but in all the wrong ways. This wasn't what she'd meant.

She tried to find ways to articulate that, but then he was kissing her, his mouth parting hers, his tongue slipping inside, tangling with her tongue, his dominance never in doubt, her submission sadly also a *fait accompli*, because when he touched her she ignited and flame could not be brought to order easily. Not by Mia. She was raging out of control, all heat and explosive need, all fiery, desperate hunger, and a deep, desperate desire to believe that he *could* make everything okay.

But what if the biggest problem she faced was Luca?

Everything he was suggesting was terrifying, because Mia knew she wouldn't be able to agree to this without losing herself to him.

And knowing that he'd bought her? For a ridiculously large sum of money? She'd love him, but she'd hate him too, and she'd hate herself.

Many things in life were nuanced. She no longer believed in black and white, good and bad. In most instances, there were shades of grey. Except for this. There was clearly a right and a wrong and she had to do what was right, or she'd never be able to live with herself.

With a final, wrenching sob, she jerked herself away, glaring at him as though he'd just stabbed her, chest moving with fast, rapid movements as she breathed in and out and her lungs burned with the effort.

'Don't.' She shivered. She trembled. She searched for more words, but 'don't' was the only one she could quickly wrap her tongue around and it tripped from her mouth, over and over. 'Don't touch me. Don't ask this of me. Please, don't say it again.'

When he took a step towards her, she lifted a hand in the air and said it again. 'Don't.'

This time, he listened, eyes sparking with hers, but body still.

She struggled for breath, for thought, but finally, words came to her. 'What my father has done is stupid and wrong. I cannot fathom how he got into this mess. But I will not agree to your offer.'

'Why not?'

She shook her head, furious. 'Do you really not see, Luca? Do you not see how cheap this makes us seem? How demeaning it is to what we've shared? You are the only man I've ever made love to, the only man who's ever touched me, and now, all my memories of you, this thing, will be tainted by what you've said tonight, by what you clearly think of me.'

She stopped, waiting for him to react to that,

to say something, to demur, but he didn't, so she pushed on, her voice wobbling a little. 'Do you really think you can buy me? And for what? Some more time? A few more weeks? A month perhaps? And what do I do when it ends? When you decide you are bored of me and leave? How do I pick up my life and go on, knowing that I sold myself to you to save my father's skin?'

She could see that her words were hitting their mark. His skin paled and his eyes seemed to widen, just a fraction.

'I am not for sale,' she reiterated, finally, tilting her chin and glaring at him for the last time.

She'd come here furious and she was leaving devastated—but Mia was just glad she was leaving at all. Another moment of being kissed by Luca and she feared she would have been unable to find the strength to go. It was now or never.

But Luca was not a man to be walked out on. Not ever, and not by Mia. He wouldn't let her leave. Not without resolving this. Not without… what? He couldn't force her to stay. He'd offered her more of himself than he'd thought he'd ever freely give another person. For Mia, it turned out, he was prepared to go further out on a limb than he'd even known existed a month ago.

And he'd tried to offer a solution to her pretty significant problem.

What good could come from chasing her?

Perhaps none, but his legs carried him anyway, out of the lounge room and then his front door, onto the street, where the afternoon sun was still bright, the heat of the day powerful.

'Mia, stop.' His voice was commanding and strong. Mia's steps faltered for a moment, but then she pushed on, reaching into her bag as she went, shoulders determinedly square as she dug for her keys.

He went for her car instead, easily identifiable in his street.

'Stop.' He almost cursed. Frustration was simmering through him. He couldn't understand why she was leaving.

'No.' Her eyes zipped around the street and belatedly he recalled her fear of being seen with him, of one of her father's friends spotting them. Well, wasn't that the point of his suggestion? That they could come out of the shadows?

'Come back inside,' he said quietly. 'It's hot, and you're angry. Come and have a drink. A swim. Think about what I'm proposing.'

Her eyes jerked to his, a frown tugging at her lips, and then she shook her head, moving to the driver door of her car. 'I could think and think and think and never change my mind. It's not enough, I told you.'

'Then what is? What do you want, Mia? More money? More clothes? What?'

She stared at him with abject confusion, then paced back to stand right in front of him, her eyes narrowed as she looked up into his face. 'Please tell me, at what point in time have I ever seemed like the kind of woman who could be bought? Do you believe, for even one moment, that financial considerations would lead me to give myself to you?'

This was coming out all wrong. It wasn't what he'd meant. Of course their relationship existed separately from any financial deal he made with her father. He simply wanted her to stay.

'I saw my mother destroyed by a man who wasn't honest with her.' His voice was raw. 'I'm just…trying to tell you what I can give you, so we both know where we stand.'

'I know where I stand,' she muttered. 'And right now, it's directly opposite an A-grade jackass.'

Pulling on her handbag strap, she looked down the street as an older couple began to promenade the length.

She stiffened, turned her attention back to Luca. 'I'm leaving now. Don't follow me. Don't call me. Don't… Just let me go.'

Letting her go was important. After all, she couldn't be any clearer about what she wanted, so what choice did he have? It ran contrary to every fibre of his being, though, and as he watched her drive away, he felt as though he was missing something important, something that he could have said or done to change her mind. But Luca Cavallaro, with all the events that had shaped him into the man he was now, was incapable of recognising the one gift he possessed that Mia wanted—the one thing he could have offered her that would have convinced her to stay. Not for a month, but for the rest of her life.

'You came.'

Luca had expected Carrick Stone to be frail, but he hadn't been prepared for just how tiny his father would seem, huddled in the large hospital bed, those sharp eyes following Luca across the room.

'You sound almost as surprised as I feel.'

Luca was rewarded by the hint of his father's smile. As a teenager, he'd wanted to impress his father, for a time, until he'd realised it was almost impossible.

'I am glad.'

Luca nodded once. A thousand feelings were bubbling inside him and yet there was a pervasive numbness too, a lack of feeling he'd been navigating ever since Mia had walked out of his life. Because if he let himself feel anything, it would overwhelm him. He knew that. Self-preservation had kicked in. He didn't think about her, he didn't talk about her, he sure as hell didn't think about her impending marriage to Lorenzo di Angelo, because that thought made him want to set the world on fire.

'Sit.'

Even now, Carrick's voice was commanding. Luca lifted a single brow, contemplated refusing, then bowed to his better nature, moving to the leather chair near the top of Carrick's bed.

'How are you?' Luca asked, even when the answer was a foregone conclusion.

'Brilliant. Fit as a fiddle,' Carrick said, eyes sparking with his dry sense of humour, so now it was Luca who found a vague smile tightening his mouth. 'Max told you about the state of my affairs?'

Luca dipped his head once, so he didn't see Carrick's hand reach out, wasn't aware of the gesture until his long, pale fingers curved around Luca's forearm.

'I want you to have it. I want you to be a part of the business.' He hesitated. 'I've wanted that for a long time, son. I just didn't know how to explain.'

'You've told me,' Luca said quietly, the touch on his arm strangely soothing.

'That is not the same as explaining.' Carrick

paused to cough. Luca waited, his heart tight-ening at his father's evident pain. 'When you walked out on me, on us, I was so angry, Luca. I was angry and hurt. My pride was hurt. You were my son and I had offered you everything I possessed, but you didn't want it.'

Luca's jaw tightened. There was such famil-iarity in that sentence, such an overlap with how Luca had been feeling lately, that he couldn't help but sit up straighter. Perhaps Carrick mis-took that for a gesture of withdrawal because he pulled his hand back, settled it in his lap.

'It took me a long time to realise that it was my fault. Blaming you was easier.' He laughed softly, shook his head, but there was sadness in his face. 'But I was wrong. I didn't know how to be with you. I never did. You're different from Max. Max I held as a baby, watched learn to walk. I know I messed up there, too, but I was never afraid of him like I was you.'

'Afraid of me?' Luca repeated.

'You arrived so angry. So sad and angry. You blamed me for everything.'

Luca bit back his rejoinder: that Carrick had deserved it. And out of nowhere, he heard Mia's words, her voice so soft against his ear but so loud inside his heart that he started.

'People aren't just good, or just bad.'

Luca had simplified things to a fault by casting his father as a villain. As a teenager, he'd seen only his father's errors, but hadn't extended compassion to the toll circumstances must have taken on Carrick. He'd never shown it to the boys, but that didn't mean he hadn't felt it.

Luca reached out, put a hand on his father's and shivered, because for a moment he felt as though Mia were with him, guiding his hand, filling him with compassion and understanding. Her wisdom had changed him. She had changed him, in so many fundamental ways.

Something clogged his throat. He looked away, angling his face until he had a better grip on his emotions.

'I know I have no right to ask.' The words were gruff. 'And I know you have your own business.' A sound, a garbled noise. 'I am very proud of you, Luca. I have tried to tell you that so many times over the years but pride always held me back. I am glad I got to say it before— the end.'

Luca's eyes felt sore. He ran a hand over them.

'If you do not want your share of the company, sign it over to Max. He knows there is a possibility of that. But I hope—we both hope— you will consider stepping into your birthright. It would mean…everything to me.'

The emotions that were strangling Luca were

too profound to unravel. He simply nodded, because he didn't trust his voice to speak.

Allegedly, it was winter in the northern tip of Australia, but it felt nothing like it, and Luca was glad. The last thing he needed was that the weather should emulate his grey mood. Sydney had been sunny too, though Luca had only stayed in the city for a few hours. Long enough to see Carrick, to have some of his most fundamental life views altered by the older man. And despite the healing that had begun—and it was indeed a healing, of such long-held wounds Luca hadn't even realised they existed: they were simply a part of him—he couldn't shake the foul mood that was heavy upon him.

His father's ill health had rattled him more than he'd expected but it was more than that.

Some of Carrick's words had dug deep into Luca and resonated with his own feelings. Pride had stopped Carrick from being honest about his feelings. What if pride had stopped Luca from understanding, let alone conveying, what he really wanted from Mia?

But what was that?

And did it even matter? She was going to marry another man, despite what he'd offered. But what had he offered that could possibly tempt her to stay with Luca? She was right.

He'd cheapened everything, had created the impression that there was something transactional about their relationship, instead of... Here, he floundered, because describing what he shared with Mia was overwhelmingly difficult.

'Drink?' Max strode onto the wrap-around balcony of the old timber house holding two beers, one extended further, for Luca.

He took it with a nod of thanks, cracked the lid and leaned forward, forearms against the railings.

'What do you think?'

Luca didn't want to tell his brother what he thought. In the days since arriving, he'd managed to avoid mentioning Mia, even though she was at the forefront of his mind constantly. Even his sleep was filled with her, his dreams flooded by Mia, so waking was always the nightmare, because she wasn't there when he reached for her.

But she could have been.

If she'd agreed to his proposition, she could have been at his side here in Australia, seeing this strange, exotic place with its unrivalled natural beauty, the outback and the bush and then this tropical paradise on the coastal fringe, with an ocean as startlingly clear as those of the Mediterranean, and huge, prehistoric-seeming trees in all directions.

Instead, she was on the other side of the globe, likely losing sleep over her father's financial mismanagement and her marriage into the di Angelo family.

'Luca?'

He grunted.

'Okay, that's it.' Max's tone was sharp. Luca had generally only heard him employ this voice when chastising his daughter, Amanda—and even then, only occasionally. 'I've had enough. What the hell is going on with you?'

Luca turned his gaze on his brother, heart racing.

'At first, I cut you some slack, because I know how seeing the old man gets to you. But not like this. This is different. So? Mind telling me why you're acting like a bear with a sore head?' He paused. 'Even more so than usual.'

Luca grunted again.

'I've never seen you like this.'

Luca took a long draw of his beer, turned his gaze back to the ocean. He wouldn't talk to Max about her. He couldn't. Not only did Luca lack the emotional experience to explain what he was feeling, he had no experience with the words needed to adequately convey his despair, and an insufficient understanding of the situation to elucidate, in any event.

'Let's start with something small.' Max

swapped to a cajoling tone. 'Tell me where you were last weekend.'

Out of nowhere, Luca's mind was flooded with images. Mia. His beach. His pool. His bedroom. His kitchen. Sitting on the edge of the table eating sun-warmed strawberries. Lying on her stomach on the tiles of the pool, reading a novel. Laughing as he drove them, her tanned legs always catching his attention, and also her easy smile. Mia's eyes—happy, shining with the force of a thousand suns, and stormy, sad, as they'd been at his home in Palermo, the last time he'd seen her. Mia, sitting beside him as he'd played the piano, listening to him talk about his family, his father, offering gentle, wise counsel. Mia, acting as though she would always be there for him.

'Luca? Answer the damned question.'

'I was in San Vito Lo Capo.'

'And were you there alone?'

Luca dropped his head forward, grief finally cracking him apart, so he felt as though he'd been drawn an awful, almighty blow to the chest. 'No.' His gut hurt. 'I was with someone.' And suddenly, he was desperate to say her name, despite everything he'd been doing to avoid this conversation. He needed to say it, like an incantation. To get her out of his head, finally. 'Mia.'

And then, despite all the reasons for his inability to explain, he found the words tumbling out of him, the whole story. Their engagement, what he'd discovered, what he'd thought a year ago when he'd gleefully avoided the wedding, how wrong he'd been, how he'd wanted her only because she was suddenly someone he couldn't have, at least, that was what he'd thought, at first. But he'd been wrong about that, too. He'd wanted Mia all for herself, for the woman she was, the woman he'd met a year ago, who'd worked her way into his mind and stayed there. But she'd worked herself into more than his mind: she was everywhere inside him, a part of his genetic make-up now.

And finally, he relayed the offer he'd made, his suggestion that he would help her father, because he'd been so desperate to keep her in his life. So desperate not to let her go off and marry another man.

'I see,' was all Max said, some time later as the sun dipped lower in the sky. From inside the house, Amanda's voice came to them.

'Daddy? Zio?'

Luca's heart clutched. *Zio.* Uncle. He'd never wanted children of his own, but his niece was an incredible person. He couldn't imagine life without her.

'I have to get Amanda's dinner.'

'Wait.' Luca held the now-empty beer bottle in both hands. 'You haven't told me what you think.'

Max considered his brother for a long time. 'Do you really want my advice?'

That was a strange question. Luca wasn't in the business of asking anyone for their opinion. But he nodded, slowly.

'You do realise I'm hardly an expert in the relationship stakes?' Max pointed out with a grimace. After all, Max's marriage to Amanda's mother had been a trainwreck from day one. Luca had urged his brother to rethink the whole idea, because clearly marriage was a fool's errand unless there was a very specific business purpose behind it, but Max had been adamant. To him, the fact a baby was on the way had meant marriage was the only option.

But they'd made each other miserable. Amanda's mother, Lauren, had drunk too much, partied too hard, and eventually died while out partying.

Luca, though, was just desperate enough to throw himself on his brother's mercy regardless, because he could see no possible option to fix a damned thing—and nor could he understand if he even wanted to fix things. After all, to what end? 'Tell me what I can do. Tell me. Anything. God, anything.'

Max stared at his brother long and hard and,

finally, laughed, tilting his head back and letting the sound crack into the evening air. 'You really don't know?'

Luca hated asking for advice almost as much as he despised being laughed at. He scowled at Max.

'Forget about it. Forget I asked.'

'You didn't ask.' Max sobered. 'I offered. So let me state what is patently obvious. Mia was upset that you propositioned her. What she wanted was a proposal. A real one, this time, not because of her father's business, but because you're in love with her.'

Luca shook his head, dismissing the appraisal immediately. 'Ridiculous. You of all people know me better than that.'

'I know you have always avoided relationships that have the potential to get serious. I know you hate the idea of loving anyone, because it means you need them, and it exposes you to a loss and rejection you've felt before. When your mother died, you were still a kid, Luca. You had everything pulled out from under you, and you never really recovered, so you push everyone away, all the time. Except...' He hesitated, shook his head. 'You've let Mia in, and now, it's done. You're in love. And so's she. It's stupid and needlessly cruel to both of you to continue pushing her away.'

Luca was very still, staring at the ocean, as

Max's words threaded through his consciousness. If he was in any doubt regarding his own feelings, then the unmistakable burst of euphoria he felt accompanied by the swift blast of fear convinced him.

'How do you know?'

'Because if she didn't love you, she wouldn't have been so infuriated by your offer. Which was really, really stupid, by the way. Totally beneath you. Another clear sign that you'd lost your mind to love.'

Luca ground his teeth, wanting to deny the charge, to point out how fanciful the entire idea was, but Max had a very annoying habit of being able to put things into perspective for Luca. Until recently, he'd been the only person on earth who Luca had listened to, whose opinion he truly valued. And now, there was also Mia.

'I've royally messed up, haven't I?'

'Yes.'

Luca cursed into the night air.

'*Zio!*' A scandalised Amanda stood behind them, looking stern and cranky, and then her little face broke into a broad smile. 'Put a dollar in the swear jar!'

Max grinned at his daughter. 'Honey, would you go and call Reg?'

'Uh-huh. What for?'

'Tell him Luca's going to need a ride to the airstrip.'

'Oh, no, already?' Amanda's face fell.

'Yes, already.' Max's voice was adamant. 'But with any luck, he'll be back soon.' He grinned. 'And he might even bring a friend.'

Except, it wasn't that simple. The entire flight back to Italy, Luca tried to work out what to say, how to say it, how best to achieve what he wanted, and every time he drew a complete blank, because understanding how he felt, why he'd said what he'd said, put a completely different spin on things.

So too did the knowledge that he loved her, and he might have made her hate him, for real, and for good.

As the flight came in to land, and his eyes traced the familiar outline of his beloved country, he realised that there was one place he could start, a small way he could *show* Mia that he hadn't meant a word of the bargain he'd tried to make.

'You cannot be serious.' Gianni Marini stared at Luca as though he'd sprouted two additional heads, one with a tail coming out of the top. He shoved the cheque back across the table. 'I will not accept it.'

Luca marvelled at the other man's pride, in the face of clearly impending destitution. Then again, hadn't he recently had a crash course in pride and the mistakes it could lead a person to make? 'Yes, you will, and we both know it.' Luca prowled to the windows, frowning as he looked down on the garden, imagining Mia here, all the years of her life since moving to Italy. His heart skipped a beat. 'It's not a gift.'

'Then what is it?'

'A year ago, I saw the potential of your company, and I still see it.'

'You also saw the ruinous state of it,' Gianni said, sitting down in his chair, head in hands. 'I don't know what to do.'

Luca felt something like pity roll through him. The older man's desperation was hard to miss, and in that moment he saw Gianni Marini as Mia did. Imperfect, but not all bad. Just misguided. But his mistakes had been formed out of love—for Mia, and a company that was part of a rich family legacy.

Even good people make bad decisions.

'But I do.'

'What?'

'I have a full business proposal to discuss with you, but now isn't the time.'

'You know what the company's worth. If you

wait a month, you can get it in a fire sale. I'm going to declare bankruptcy.'

Luca stiffened.

'What?'

'The di Angelo merger is off.'

Luca's brain was pulsing so hard he felt that his head might explode. His next question was heavy with the weight of all his hopes. 'And the marriage?'

'Another failure. It was a failure from the start. What did I do to deserve this?'

Luca thrust his hands onto his hips, hearing the older man's question and disregarding it. Didn't he realise that this was turning into one of the best days of Luca's life? It was imperative now that he find Mia. He needed to speak to her, immediately. If there was any chance this was because of him...

But of course it wasn't.

Far more likely, Gianni had come to his senses and pulled out of the merger, and, as a result, the wedding had been called off.

'What happened?'

Gianni's eyes met Luca's, then shifted away. 'Mia happened.'

Luca's heart thudded. 'Explain it to me, carefully.'

And the older man did. He told Luca that Mia had come to him, even before she knew about the state of the company's finances, to tell him she couldn't go through with the marriage. 'I don't love him.'

Luca dropped his head forward. 'When?'

'A long time ago. Weeks.'

Before she'd come to Luca that night, so furious. 'And you told her about the business's dire situation?'

Gianni paled. 'I wanted to change her mind. It was selfish of me. So selfish.'

Desperate people do desperate things.

Luca had reflected on that himself, when in a more compassionate mood.

So even that night, she'd known she wouldn't marry di Angelo, and that her father's business would crumble, and still she hadn't thought twice about accepting his offer. Because she loved him too much? Was it possible that Max was right? She would have sooner seen her father go bankrupt than agree to Luca's terms.

Luca felt as though he were drowning and the only way he knew how to grab a life raft was to focus on his purpose for coming here today. 'I'm taking over Marini Enterprises,' he said with a determined nod. 'And when I ask you this next question, you're going to understand why it makes crystal-clear sense for me to do so.' After all, it was a family business, and Luca had every intention of becoming just that: a family, with Mia.

CHAPTER ELEVEN

IT HAD ALWAYS been difficult for Mia to choose which flavour of gelato she preferred. Sometimes, it was strawberry, other times hazelnut, and then there were afternoons when only the richest, most sinfully indulgent chocolate would do. But this was an afternoon for the trifecta, the holy grail of sensations, rich and comforting at the same time.

She dug her spoon into the combination of three heavenly flavours, savouring it as she weaved through the crowded Palermo streets, head bent to avoid meeting the eyes of anyone she might know, or that her parents might know.

Another broken engagement behind her, the news had been announced by the di Angelo family and spread like wildfire.

It was Mia's worst nightmare.

At least, she'd thought it was, until her worst nightmare had morphed into reality and she'd had to endure the offence of Luca's offer followed quickly by the reality of losing him—and knowing a life without him in it.

She'd tossed and turned at night, wondering if she was crazy to have refused his offer.

It was offensive and barbaric and wrong but, just as he'd said, being together was right, and maybe there was even enough rightness between them to justify her accepting his proposal.

But she couldn't.

It would have been impossible to live with herself, and with him.

To be discarded by him when it suited, to know that fate awaited her. How could he have asked it of Mia?

But then, weren't all relationships a gamble? Marrying someone didn't ensure you wouldn't be discarded. Loving someone didn't either— look at his mother. So maybe there really was no hope? Tears, her constant companion since that night, sparkled on her lashes and she didn't bother to check them. Instead, she threw sunglasses on and continued to eat her ice cream, one small scoop at a time, hoping that the sugar rush would do its job any moment now and make Mia feel, for a while at least, a little better.

Her car was parked by a fountain in the square. She scanned for traffic, waiting for a speeding Vespa to pass, then walked over the road, keys held in her hand as she approached. She almost didn't see him at first. Between the hot afternoon sun, the ice cream and trying to unlock her old car without spilling said ice cream, Mia quite literally had her hands full. But then a movement, a familiar shift, caught Mia's attention and she looked across to see Luca Cavallaro standing, feet planted hip-width apart, hands in pockets, eyes watching her. Studying her.

And she was a crying mess.

Great.

Just great.

'Mia.' His voice growled out of him, barrelling towards her, and she flinched, because she wasn't ready for this. She was emotionally exhausted. She still hadn't recovered from their last interaction; she couldn't do this again.

'Luca.' She wrenched open her car door, but Luca was there, his hand on the top of the metal, his body forming a frame around hers, so she was caught between the car and him. He smelled heavenly. She swallowed, wishing her tears would stop, wishing, wishing, wishing a thousand things, all of them impossible.

'I heard about your wedding.'

She blinked. It was the last thing on her mind. Strange how right it had felt to end that engagement, compared to when things finished with Luca.

'It was the right decision.'

Luca's chest moved with the force of his breathing. 'Why didn't you tell me?'

'It wasn't relevant.'

'To us?'

She bit down on her lip and shook her head.

'Do you regret it?'

She blinked, the question strange. Why would he even ask that? 'No.'

'I'm glad.'

She angled her face away, focusing on the fountain with its rapidly falling water splashing over the side onto the footpath.

'I had been torturing myself, you know, imagining you preparing for the wedding, getting ready to become another man's wife. I thought I might stay in Australia. Move there permanently.'

She swallowed hard.

'How could I come back to Italy, to know myself within reach of you, and never touch you again?'

Her heart splintered. 'I'm not getting married, but it doesn't change anything. I'm not for sale, Luca.'

'You never were.' He pressed his thumb to her chin, drawing her face to meet his. 'I was completely wrong to make that proposition. I was desperate not to lose you, desperate to help you, but it was still one of the dumbest things I've ever said. I'm very, very sorry.'

Until he spoke those words, Mia hadn't realised quite how badly she'd needed to hear them. Thinking he believed her capable of what he'd suggested had been a heavy burden.

'The thing is, until I travelled to the other side of the world, I didn't quite understand why I'd reacted that way.'

A drop of gelato melted over the edge of the cup, landing on her thumb. She lifted it to her mouth without thinking, tasting the sweetness. His eyes dropped to her lips, stared at her there, and her stomach did a thousand somersaults.

'Luca,' she whispered, a plea. 'This has to stop.' A lump formed in her throat. 'You can't keep doing this to me. You keep turning up, and making me think—'

'Think what, *cara*?'

But how could she admit that to him? He wasn't the only one who was afraid of being vulnerable. 'You can't keep acting as if this, us, as if there's something more here. I realised very early on that we want different things in life, so continuing to act as though we're in lockstep or something…it's torture. This has to stop.'

'But what if that's not true, Mia? What if it turns out we both want exactly the same thing?'

She shook her head, the cruelty of the question landing square between her ribs. 'Don't,' she cried, clutching the gelato cup hard, needing to hold onto something.

'I thought I didn't want children. I was adamant on that score. But the truth is, I'd just never met anyone I cared about enough to want to have a family with—the idea of loving terrified me, until I loved and lost. Now? The idea of being with you, of making a family with you, fills me with a joy I've never known before. For you to carry *my* child? It is all I want.' His words burst through Mia with radiant energy. 'Now, the idea of having a family with you is all I care about. We are meant to be together—can't you see that?'

She shook her head, not because she didn't believe him, but because she felt as though she were in some kind of mad dream.

'Mia, listen to me,' he said, with urgency. 'I'm in love with you. That scares the hell out of me, if I'm honest, because I've never been in love before, and all my experience of relationships has shown them to be capable of wrecking a person completely. I've never desired that sort of risk—the reward wasn't there to justify it. Until now. Until I fell in love with you and realised I would walk through the very fires of hell to be with you, to be open about how much I love you, to be loved back by you, even for a short amount of time. It would be worth it. If something goes wrong and I am destroyed by this love, as I fear I would be if you were to leave me, it will still have been worth it. I'm terrified, Mia, of what loving you means, of how dangerous it is to give myself to someone like this, but it turns out, when you're in love—real, life-changing love—it's not a choice, rather than a state of being. I love you. It's that simple.'

She stared at him, completely dumbfounded. 'Luca, stop. It's okay. You don't need to say this. You don't need to do this. I'm going to be okay. I don't need you to save me, to save my family, from financial ruin.'

His response was to lean closer, his face just an inch from hers. 'I am in love with you. Every single part of me loves all the bits of you. For always.' And then, to Mia's continually expanding sense of shock, he got to his knees in the middle of the footpath, the fountain behind him, passers-by pausing to watch. Mia didn't notice any of that, though. She only had eyes for Luca.

'What I should have said, on that afternoon at my house, is that I cannot imagine my life without you in it. This is not about business, it is not about money, it is not about saving you. It is, if anything, about saving me. Do you have any idea what my life was like before you were a part of it? Mia, you are everything to me. You are the first person I think of when I wake up, the last thing I want to see at the end of my day, you are in my thoughts while I work, always. And you have been since I first met you. This last year, I couldn't get you out of my head—why is that? I barely knew you, and yet, on some level, I already loved you.'

She shook her head because it was impossible to believe him. 'Listen to me. I was so angry with you—irrationally so. I hated you for lying to me because I expected so much more of you. I think I had already started to love you, certainly to need you in my life. The second I read of your engagement to another man, I was driven crazy. It wasn't just jealousy, though, it was a need to set things to right. I just…went about it in completely the wrong way.'

She closed her eyes softly. 'Not *completely* the wrong way.'

'I berated you and, hell, I kidnapped you, Mia. I couldn't bear to lose you. I just didn't understand why that was the most fundamentally important thing in my life until I faced a lifetime of living with my mistakes, of living without you.'

'God, Luca,' she said on a half laugh, half sob. 'I have to say, this is the last thing I expected to hear today.'

'But is it something you want to hear?' He stared at her with such hope, such anxious, uncertain vulnerability that Mia could only nod at first, before adding, 'Oh, yes. Very much.'

A smile burst through his features. 'Then you

will hear it every single day. Every day. For the rest of our lives.'

Her heart burst.

'You are a part of me, Mia, and I hope, my darling, beautiful love, that you will agree to share your future with mine. Marry me. As soon as we can get a licence, please, marry me.'

Luca being Luca, the licence was expedited and their wedding held only one week later in a small church in the north of Australia, with sweeping views of a stunning tropical rainforest, accompanied by the sound of birds and waves. Unlike their first wedding, which had a guest list comprised of hundreds of Europe's wealthy elite, the church had only a handful of attendees. Mia's parents and a pair of her best friends from high school, Luca's brother and niece, and his father, who, though frail and in a wheelchair, had been flown up from Sydney and sat in the front row with a blanket over his knees despite the heat of the day, an expression on his face that Mia found so incredibly familiar it blew her away.

Luca had said that he was like his father in many ways, and they certainly looked alike—all three of them, for Max had many similarities to Luca, too, and seeing the warmth between the brothers made Mia's heart very happy. But more than that, seeing Luca with Carrick and knowing that her own words had helped bring about a reconciliation made her glow from the inside out. Because the resentment Luca had felt for his father had really only been hurting Luca, and in opening himself to love, to loving his father despite their imperfect past, he'd allowed himself to step into a happier future.

As for Amanda, Max's daughter, Mia was entirely captivated. She was a charming, precocious, intelligent and funny eight-year-old who laughed readily and helped willingly. She went out of her way to care for Mia, sitting with her before the wedding, ferrying her cups of tea, doing everything she could to ensure Mia's happiness. She would be an excellent older cousin, when the time came.

And though Mia had always known she wanted children—and she did—she wasn't in any rush. She was young, and she was, evidently, just a little selfish when it came to Luca. She found the idea of sharing him, just yet, to be something she was not yet ready for.

There'd be plenty of time for that, in due course, but, for now, she simply wanted to enjoy being Mrs Luca Cavallaro.

Their wedding reception was at a Stone family property attached to the 'pearl farm', the most beautiful beach Mia had ever seen. The house itself was nestled in amongst a rainforest with sweeping views of the coastline on one side and ancient trees the other. The wrap-around balcony was adorned with fairy lights, and a long, straight table was set up on one edge, allowing their party to enjoy dinner.

Mia was already in love with Luca, but that night she fell completely in love with this property, his family, with all the parts of him, just as he'd said he felt for her.

And seeing her parents so happy, so relaxed, gave Mia a freedom she'd never thought she'd know. They were imperfect, in many ways, and she would use her mother's style of parenting as a guide of what not to do when she had children of her own, but she was a master at accepting them as they were, for their good, their bad, their mistakes, and loving them despite that. As with Luca and Carrick, letting herself acknowledge a person's faults and then loving them anyway represented a freedom for Mia. Besides, with Luca by her side, nobody in the world had the power to hurt or wound her. She was truly, everlastingly content.

Where the business was concerned, Luca had indeed analysed the strengths and weaknesses of Marini Enterprises, and, once they returned to Palermo after a six-week honeymoon, he set about a significant restructure and rebuilding.

It would take years to return the business to its former glory, but within half a year, positive impacts were already being felt.

Eight months after returning to Palermo, Carrick Stone took a turn for the worse, and while there was always grief associated with death, there was happiness here too, because there was love. Both of Carrick's sons were by his side as he slipped from this life. It was a reconciliation none could have foreseen just one year earlier.

But in letting himself love Mia, Luca had opened himself to all kinds of love, to the risks associated with it, but also the confidence that came from being freely honest with yourself.

Mia had truly opened his eyes to a whole different way of living. His love for her grew each day.

The following year, when Mia and Luca travelled to the pearl farm for Amanda's birthday, it was with some news of their own—they gave to Amanda the best gift they could: she was going to be an older cousin.

In the end, they'd conceived quite by accident, and not learned of Mia's pregnancy until she was four months along. The surprise had been a very welcome one—by then, they were both ready. If Mia had entertained any doubts of Luca's sincerity about his desire for children, they were completely wiped away by his reaction.

'Luca, are you crying?'

'No, Mia Cavallaro,' he'd drawled, all alpha male, except for eyes that seemed, to Mia, just the tiniest bit moist. 'Now sit down immediately and prepare to spend the next five months being totally pampered.'

She laughed. 'I'm pregnant, not made of glass.'

'I don't care.' His nostrils flared. 'You are pregnant with my baby and while I cannot physically carry the baby, I can do everything else.'

'Luca?' She pressed a finger to his lips. 'I'm still me—the same person I was yesterday, who went surfing with you. Remember?'

'Cristo.' He paled. 'That was stupid.'

'No.' She laughed. 'It's fine. Everything's fine.' She reached for his hand and pressed it to her stomach. 'Everything's going to be fine.'

Nonetheless, Luca barely breathed normally for the next five months. Not only did he want their child desperately, he wanted the baby enough to make deals with God constantly, for the baby's health, for Mia's. He loved excessively, but not without fear. He couldn't bear it if anything were to happen to either of them.

They were blessed, however, with the birth of

a healthy baby girl, three weeks ahead of schedule, in the very middle of the night. A year later, a little boy joined their family and only eleven months later, another girl.

Mia had the big, loud family she'd always wanted, and while she was exhausted, she was also deliriously happy. She could never have imagined, on their first, awful wedding day, that her grief and shame could morph into these feelings of such sublime contentment. She couldn't have imagined she'd ever feel happy again, let alone know a happiness like this—and yet she did. Mia Cavallaro was truly, sincerely, blissfully content, and would be ever after...so was Luca.

But all those years earlier, on the night of their wedding, when Luca had known such incredible happiness, he found himself looking beyond his own relief, gratitude and contentment to think of another. Max Stone had been single a long time, since Amanda's mother's death, and there was a jadedness about Max that Luca had only been able to recognise since opening the floodgates to his own happiness.

He found himself looking into the night sky, at the sparkling stars, right as a single light flashed across the sky—shooting past him, inviting him to make a wish. What could a man

do, who'd already had all his own wishes ful-
filled, but press a request into the heavens for
someone else to find their own lasting, meaningful, true happy ending? And so it was that
Luca Cavallaro wished upon a star for Max to
one day know the same all-consuming love that
he, Luca, had finally been blessed with…

* * * * *

*Did you fall head over heels for
The Sicilian's Deal for "I Do"?*

*Then don't miss the next instalment in
the Brooding Billionaire Brothers duet,
coming soon!*

*In the meantime, dive into these other stories
by Clare Connelly!*

Pregnant Princess in Manhattan
The Secret She Must Tell the Spaniard
Desert King's Forbidden Temptation
The Boss's Forbidden Assistant
Twelve Nights in the Prince's Bed

Available now!